Stefanie Dawn

DEDICATION

To the brazen demon in all of us.

Lure of a DEMON

AN UNEARTHLY SINS NOVEL

CHAPTER
1

ILSA

Blood type: inconclusive.

Those words glared up at me from the report hanging limply in my hands. They're the same words these reports always showed, and while I didn't expect any different, there was still that persistent hope I'd get some answers.

Hope that was now dwindling, telling me I needed to find another way to solve this issue.

Clinical reports and tests didn't offer me any information I didn't already know or couldn't figure out through my own investigation.

Kelly had slipped me a copy of this report over drinks last night. Drinks and stilted conversation while she tried desperately to rekindle some semblance of the *relationship* we had. Prior to my asking her for help over these past few weeks, we hadn't seen each other since before my last deployment.

Kelly would say we were in a relationship back then.

My view was we were simply sleeping together.

That difference in opinion might be a clue as to why it didn't work out.

Kelly was a medical examiner for the city and one of the few people on this planet I knew would believe me when I told her what I had seen—she was all star signs, crystals, and the alignment of the planets. I had taken a gamble on her willingness to accept things she could neither see nor prove would mean she'd believe *me*.

She did, without much question or the skeptical raised brow and smirk of amusement I'd get from most other people.

I guess I should be thankful to her for at least that, and then going above and beyond and putting her job and reputation at risk to get me copies of reports that shouldn't reach civilian hands.

I had to tell someone. For while I'd seen a lot of fucked-up shit, this was hard for even me to swallow. From the poverty of the area I grew up in before my father worked his way through the army ranks, to the horrors I'd witnessed while on deployment myself, I'd absorbed it all.

But I still struggled to explain the incident a few months ago.

Perhaps that was part of the problem—I was trying to explain the unexplainable.

I wouldn't say it was the worst thing I'd ever seen, but it was the only incident that occurred on home soil that haunted my dreams.

It was a little over two months ago, and I'd decided to drink away my sorrows for at least one night following the finality of my medical discharge from the military.

By the way, it didn't help—the alcohol—and it's not a path I've gone down since.

The last thing I needed on top of my already damaged body was alcohol poisoning or some other weak shit which would get me sent to a hospital again. I'd spent enough time within hospitals and rehabilitation centers to last a lifetime—several lifetimes in fact.

For all the good it did.

As if to remind me of the injury I was already overly aware of, a pang of sharp pain, gone as quickly as it had come, radiated from my leg.

Yes, I know I was weaker after the injury than before, and yes, I've been forcefully reminded of my humanity and limitations.

Thank you very much for the reminder, *body*.

But despite the alcohol and the anger-fueled thoughts that raged through my mind as I slammed empty glass after empty glass on the bar, the bartender continued to serve me when he probably shouldn't.

When *she* walked into the bar, it was hard not to notice her.

Deep red hair was styled loosely around her shoulders in those waves I never understood how girls got to work, not that I'd ever been one of those girls to try too hard to get my hair to do anything other than whatever the hell it felt like. Tight leather pants and a corset to match sculpted her already toned body, and dark makeup shadowed her eyes, adding an extra layer of mystery.

And damn me, an extra layer of fuckability.

She might as well have had the word *trouble* stamped across her forehead.

But her eyes, I'd never seen eyes like hers before. Irises of gold and yellow shined with a promise of danger and sexual prowess. Although perhaps the last bit was only in my head.

I also hadn't been laid since before my injury, and occasionally my body would get the better of my mind, and my usually otherwise trained thoughts would stray. With *her,* I blamed the haze of alcohol pushing its way through my veins, making me blink through the blur as I stared at her, mentally wandering my hands over her body.

Yeah, it was a pig move, and I never usually viewed women as purely sexual beings. I cared who they were inside. All aspects of their personality were much more important than what they looked like. But there was something about her which almost called for it like she knew exactly what everyone in the bar was thinking, and beyond that, she *wanted* them to think it.

But her eyes said *keep your hands off.*

Trouble.

Shooting me a look that would've had me staggering if I weren't sitting down, she flawed me and set off a reaction of desire I'd rather forget.

Because I had more self-control than that.

The alcohol had provided me with just enough relaxation to create a light buzz in my mind, but not enough to stop me from defending myself if I needed to.

With her, I didn't know if I'd need to defend myself or if I wanted to take her to bed.

Or both.

There was no shortage of women to seduce in the military. Women who whether or not they had come out or they were simply curious about being with another woman, and would've happily slept with me. But I didn't really want anyone after my injury. There was in the deep recesses of my mind, the awareness I might not be able to move as gracefully in the bedroom as I had before, that my leg might give out or stunt my motion, and it might be a turn-off for women.

Weakness was certainly a turn-off for me, and I didn't want a pity fuck.

In fact, I didn't want anyone until I saw *her* move.

I'd love to say I witnessed her dancing, and that's how I knew she could move so smoothly.

Instead, she had kicked the living shit out of almost everyone in the bar.

This woman was something else.

It turns out she was *literally* something else.

She started a fight at the bar, I had no idea why. But she'd proved to be more than capable of looking after herself.

Her strength was almost supernatural.

Funny about that.

I had considered getting involved but decided against it. I figured I'd done enough fighting for a while, and instead, I opted to simply leave her to whatever shit she was dealing with which made her start a bar fight in the first place. The fact she was outnumbered was her problem.

It turns out it wasn't a problem.

My conscience would've kicked in if I believed her to be in danger of getting hurt—protect the innocent rang strong in me—and these men in their bikie vests, well, I doubted they were innocent. But she was barely cracking a sweat as she took down two of the larger men, so I shrugged and moved to leave. As I was making my way toward the front door, I glanced back at her, maybe for one last look, maybe because the horny part of me wanted something to think about when I collapsed in bed tonight, or maybe because she was magnetic and I couldn't keep my eyes off her and her movements.

Her shoulders heaved with deep heavy breaths as she stood over her latest victim, and a wide grin plastered on her face exposed teeth slightly sharper than I'd have expected.

The part that really got my attention—swiveling her head to look back at me before I left, her eyes were yellow—no longer golden, but bright yellow with black slits for irises.

Maybe I could've played that alone off as a trick of the light. However, the veins on her neck and arms had grown so dark I could trace their pathways across her body, black lines filled with ink spilling out underneath her milky skin in random spots that seemed to take her over, changing the tone of her skin to a sickly gray before it became black in places. It was like she was being painted from the inside out into something not distinctly human.

I had seen a lot of things.

Her victim stirred, and she silenced him with a kick to the head before she stared back at me, her head snapping up with an unnatural speed, and I know she knew I had *seen* her.

Yet, she smiled.

Most other people would tell themselves they were crazy, and it couldn't possibly be real. But I know what I saw.

I know what I saw.

Since then, I'd been following her path of destruction across the city. I knew it was her after the first few attacks occurred. Several times I had tried to be in the right place at the right time by chance, but it hadn't worked, not yet. I didn't have enough data to create a pattern yet. The signs were the same—occupants of the buildings were beaten until they fled and the buildings destroyed. No one wanted to talk to the police about what happened because it would start a line of awkward questioning about who would want to target them and what they were doing in those places. Was it really only a bar? A club? What was in the rooms out back? Evidence of drug labs was denied, and the ownership of the buildings was so expertly twisted up in paperwork it was obviously the work of some larger criminal organization. Or several.

And her motivations were even more of a mystery. Was she working for someone or attacking at random?

Then there was the constant insistence by the victims they never saw the attacker. Which seems so unlikely it bordered on impossible. It eventually clicked in my mind it was code for *a girl beat us up, and we didn't want to admit it.*

Kelly had been an invaluable source of information, but part of me knew Kelly was only helping because she hoped to get back together with me. I chose to ignore that part because then I could also ignore the guilt reminding me I was practically using her, and not only for sex this time.

So, this red-headed woman, this otherworldly being, this fucking monster or whatever she was, had targeted gang clubhouses, homes of pimps, biker gang headquarters, and fronts for drug labs and money laundering. This couldn't be an accident. She knew what she was doing and the sort of places she was targeting. It would be too much of a coincidence for her to simply happen across these places each time she decided it was time to fuck something up.

I shouldn't be concerned. Those people had made their own bed and perhaps got what was coming to them. If it weren't from her, then it was bound to be someone else who took them down, right? But she was careless and reckless, and with every move she made, the chances of someone innocent getting hurt or killed multiplied exponentially.

Someone in the wrong place at the wrong time.

Collateral damage.

Unacceptable.

Besides, Kelly advised the police were aware there was growing tension within the underground crime sanctions in the city, each group blaming the others for the damage. Something was going to break soon, and if I didn't get to her, then certainly those whose toes she was stepping on would find her first.

Or kill each other, again with the potential for the loss of innocent lives.

I was no novice. I knew the crime-circles ran this city, tending to leave alone the rich-bitch side of the city and keeping to this end, where they could pay off cops and get away with it.

But we come back to the same point—protect the innocent.

Despite what this woman was doing, I don't think I wanted her to end up in the hands of those who would kill her. She gave the impression there was at least some level of integrity with the places and people she chose to unleash herself upon. Or perhaps she was simply a tool, being led by someone else. Either way, she didn't deserve to die.

On top of that—and this one bothered me a lot because a creature with sharp teeth, yellow eyes, and black inky skin surely couldn't have ethics—but for whatever reason, she never seemed to kill anyone. Not once, although she'd put more than a few of them in the hospital. It was as though she lived by some fucked-up code where she was happy to maim people and destroy places as long as she didn't actually kill anyone.

Weird rules, but psychopaths often had their own set of rules, I guess.

She was more than a psychopath, though. I know

what I saw. Something else, something not human—no fingerprints, untraceable blood they were unable to identify the type, and strength beyond what should be possible for her size.

After a while, when the police reports and public information were getting me nowhere, I added some of my own research into my investigation.

Inky skin, sharp teeth, yellow eyes.

Demon.

Whoever she was, she was unnatural, and I would find her.

So, after the experience at the bar and the reports of similar happenings, I had asked Kelly for copies of police reports for anything with unusual results, and unidentifiable blood certainly counted as unusual. I think Kelly took the results personally, as though being unable to identify demon blood as a type was some insult to her career and abilities in her profession.

Kelly hadn't wanted to help me further, scared to get involved and put her career at risk any more than she already had. Understandable. I preferred to work alone anyway. Apart from the risk she could lose her job, we hadn't exactly left on the best of terms, but I fed her some drivel about needing to find purpose in my life since my discharge.

I didn't want to admit to myself it wasn't a lie.

On top of that, because it was still, and would always be, my duty to protect the innocent, I realized no cops were going to believe that not only was there was a connection between these incidents beyond the gang wars, but the connection was a toned red-headed woman on a warpath who happened to be an otherworldly being.

Demon.

I'm not sure what more proof I was waiting for to act, and to find a solution. Even if I were wrong, the worst-case scenario was I spend a bit of time trying to convince myself I'm not crazy, and perhaps as a bonus, apprehend someone who's putting innocent lives in danger.

But my mother told me about *Guahaioque.*

So, I had more research to do.

Real demons living in the city

It felt stupid even to type it into the search bar, but I had to start somewhere, I guess. I blinked as I clicked, and the results filled the screen. Most of them weren't helpful—a few band names and movies, an article about exorcisms being on the rise—*I'll come back to that one*—and the usual fandom pages for movies and television series involving demons and the supernatural.

There were a lot of those.

Unperturbed, I continued scrolling, even hitting on the rarely used *next page* button to see more results. It was here I found something interesting. A blog targeting my city, my home, with theories there were not only demon sightings within the city, but there was an entire demon population living amongst us without our knowledge.

Interesting.

Unsettling.

Clicking the link, I scrolled through the blog's discussion, which had an increasing number of contributors over the past five years, and the discussion continued to be active up to only last week. I read the most recent entries.

> *I swear to God my old CEO was a demon, the man oozed sexual prowess, and I swear he could make women orgasm just by looking at him.*

Sounds like a fun guy, but not exactly what I was searching for. Until I continued reading.

> *I had met my boyfriend for a bit of fun during my lunch break, if you know what I mean, and after my break, I needed to drop off some reports to the boss. He*

wasn't my direct boss, I worked in a different department, but I had seen him around. When I walked into his office, he looked up before I had even knocked, his nostrils flared, and he tilted his chin as though he was smelling me. *He made some comment about* afternoon delight, *and I thought* oh my God, do I smell like sex? *Surely not. Then there was a flash of yellow across his eyes, and I knew I didn't imagine it. I never told anybody, so when I saw other reports of people seeing yellow eyes on people, it gave me the chills. I always got weird vibes from that guy. I quit shortly afterward. And now reading all this and people are saying there are* more *demons around the city, this is terrifying to me. I think I'm going to move.*

I leaned back in my chair and stared at the computer screen, tapping a pen against my chin. Something like this could easily be discarded as the ravings of a woman who had an overactive imagination, but given all the other examples, and exactly as she had mentioned, so many others had all seen the yellow eyes. Including me.

I had tried to be so steadfast in my assurance to myself I wasn't crazy, but now I knew other people had seen the same thing. This meant I could tell the inner part of myself that harbored a seed of doubt, I definitely *hadn't* imagined it. All these people, without any prior connection to each other, all reported the same thing and in several areas across the city. This city. *My* city. All different people with yellow eyes—CEOs, everyday laborers, people in nightclubs—this couldn't be ignored.

I tapped out a reply to the poster.

> *I'm ex-military, and I'm trying to investigate all these reports. Can you tell me where you worked or at least what area of the city the business is located?*

I left it at that, short and simple.

I couldn't sit here staring at the screen waiting for a reply, so I moved on to research in another tab, typing...

How to kill a demon

CHAPTER 2

RAY

Finding the perfect combination, it was hard not to laugh at the fact other demons hadn't figured it out yet. How stupid can they be?

Did I walk around the apartment I broke into last night and sing loudly about how smart I was? Maybe.

Of course, I had heard the tales of demons who had come to the surface, promptly lost control of their cover, killed one or several people, and had been returned to Hell, never to have another chance at life on the surface. There had been other stories too, the rarer ones where a demon had killed a human without consequences, when they had lost control and were worse than animals, being left to go free after they had killed.

Some thought this meant we were no more than

pawns for God to use.

I wasn't so sure.

But all that was well above my pay grade, and frankly above my care factor now, and being sent back to Hell without the chance of another surface visit wasn't a risk I was willing to take. Besides, humans were like little pets, weren't they? Kind of cute and helpless. Unless they were actively trying to kill me, I had no real reason to kill them first.

Pawns of God? I don't think by any stretch of the imagination what I'm doing could be considered *God's work.*

But I had figured it out, cracked it, found a way to have the best of both worlds.

If I caused all the destruction I wanted—got into fights and allowed my bloodlust the freedom to explore Earth, even in controlled circumstances—I could get away with it.

But if—and this was the key—if, and only if, I kept it directed at the *right* people—the criminals, the low-lifes, and the ones who hurt other humans. The pimps and gang members, the drug dealers and cooks-of-all-things-illegal, rapists, and suspected murderers—people who were the worst of humanity.

They had made their choices to do what they were doing, and if I had my fun with them, well, then there were no consequences.

As long as I didn't kill them.

So, I've been tearing down their places of business where all they do is hurt other people, putting the people who work there in their place before burning their businesses to the ground. How can God be mad at that?

I'm helping but for selfish reasons.

It's a win-win.

Like being a kid in a candy store, everything is new and fun. I'm unsupervised—there are very few rules—and I can let loose. I liked Earth more and more with every day that passed. I had even stopped going home between bouts and started sleeping here. Rather than popping up every couple of weeks, I'd been here for a few days straight now, and dammit, if I weren't inclined to stay. They wouldn't miss me—it's not like family values ran strong through demons. Besides, I was replaceable—one of thousands could step in and take my place to torture the guilty in Hell.

The Silver City might have to start paying more attention, perhaps rein us in somehow as it seemed more and more demons were being enticed by the lure of life on Earth. Few stayed very long, though, but no one monitored who was here and for how long. We were basically free to roam and do as we pleased.

Something about that felt almost inherently wrong, like we should be guided by some sort of rules from the Big Man upstairs since we were in *his* playground of Earth. His own little science experiment.

Or however it was he viewed humanity—*his children?* I don't know. I'd never spoken to him.

Much like I'd never spoken to the Devil either, and I never would. I was only a low-level demon, after all.

Back to the theory that our being present on Earth served a purpose, and in some twisted way maybe we were *meant* to be exactly where we were, at any given time, whether the reason was apparent or not. Demons were as much a part of the system as humans and angels, all working together and playing our part in some grand plan no one else could see but God himself.

Pawns.

I hated the idea. Some cosmic fate I had no control over? Fuck that.

But the reasoning had somewhat led me to my current path, and I can't be punished if I'm technically not hurting anyone innocent, right?

Technicalities, my favorite.

Sometimes, like tonight, I liked to change things up. Rather than simply stroll in and turn the place upside-down, I might do a little roleplay of the non-kinky—and therefore arguably less fun—sort. I was relatively muscular but slender enough if I wasn't flexing, I could go almost unnoticed and assumed to be non-threatening. But it didn't take a genius to figure out if you divert people's attention away from your fit form built for fighting and direct their eyes to your tits, they were less likely to be observant where they should be.

Less likely to see the trouble coming.

Tonight, I stumbled into the clubhouse. It was an intentional stumble, but they didn't need to know that. Giggling as I gripped the doorframe, I allowed my body to swing back and forth with a slow, lazy momentum, casting my gaze around the room with equal leisure.

Twelve men, three women.

Easy.

If the dozen-odd bikes lined up in front of the building weren't enough to give away this was a biker clubhouse, then the matching vests and patches of all the men in the room certainly were. Criminals, nothing more. I didn't need to know anything more about them. It was our role in Hell to torture those who had sinned.

But why couldn't I bring that fun to the surface?

Within reason, of course.

Most demons saw it as a waste of time to be on Earth, and I didn't blame them. Many humans were tedious, and while it was fun to journey up and mess with them a little, those types of quick visits decreased as the novelty wore off. So, I shouldn't draw *too* much blood or cause *too* much damage, and I certainly couldn't kill.

Since I had found the balance, I knew very well the sort of fun I could have—and get away with—here in this room with these unsuspecting men.

When I had kicked the door open, they had turned with rage flaring in their eyes, several hands all flying to their belts, hovering over weapons at the ready. But relaxed as soon as they had seen me stumbling about with a false level of drunkenness, all wide-eyed and giggling, wearing a tank top which, while it appeared to be too small, was intentionally designed to show as much as possible without actually being naked.

I'll give Earth credit—there was something about the night air here, the way the cool breeze licked at my skin. There was nothing like it in Hell, and while the warmth was comforting, I hadn't ever felt as alive as I did the first time I experienced the sting of the cold evening air. Even during the summer, there was chill and calm in the night air, and it charged me.

While I had come to the surface for some fun, but now I wasn't so sure I wanted to go back. Hence, why I needed to maintain a balance with the actions I took so I'd be allowed to stay.

So far, it had worked, apparently.

If I didn't let loose to a certain point, I'd lose control, and then I'd really be in trouble. After all, I was still relatively new at containing my demon for more than a few hours at a time, and it was a steep learning curve.

Watching as the men eyed me, I smiled stupidly and ran my teeth over my bottom lip.

"Oopsie!" I cried, adding an extra octave to my voice which wouldn't naturally be there. "Looks like I'm in the wrong place."

As I turned to leave, I slipped, and, as suspected, a strong arm swung under me, catching me around the shoulders and pulling me to my feet. It would've been a move of gallantry if it weren't for the way he immediately pressed me against his side, taking his free hand and running his fingers down my neck and over the tops of my breasts.

Fucking bold of him.

Also, bit of a dick move if he thought I was as drunk as I was pretending to be.

Don't get me wrong, I had downed half a bottle of whiskey. I loved the burn of it sliding down my throat and then the slow heat as it settled in my stomach. The cheaper the bottle, the better. But I was still in complete control.

I was in complete control is what I told myself.

Even as I noticed my sight blurred slightly before it cleared again after my near fall, the rush of blood to my head obscured my vision with the assistance of the alcohol.

Okay, so maybe it was more like a full bottle, and maybe that was poor judgment on my behalf. Still, I was certain I could take everyone in this bar.

I wasn't here for them anyway, not really. They were a means to an end to get out the lust for violence that lived within my veins.

But once I had them cleared out, whether they walked or dragged themselves by their fingers, would depend on how much of a fight they put up, then I could destroy the clubhouse. I'd developed a bit of a taste for arson—for some reason, I felt comfortable with flames, funny that—and I figured if they don't have a place to action the crime, then crime would be reduced.

I got my kicks, bad guys lost, and I'm not being a wimp about it. Everybody wins.

"Watch your hands there, buster..." I purred as I looked at him, "... you just might lose them."

He laughed, and I actually flinched when he grabbed my breast in his hand, palming it roughly. I cocked an eyebrow at him, but he wasn't looking at my face. He was too busy watching the motion of my flesh under his hand, jiggling my breast obscenely. Did he really think women derived pleasure from his fumbling? I suppose he didn't really care.

His other hand was still clamped firmly against my hip, pressing me against his side.

"Maybe you should be careful where you wander into, girly." He snickered, slapping lightly at my breast. I frowned at him. He was taking *way* too many liberties with this act I was putting on, and

I'm sure a vein in my neck was twitching at the effort not to break his hand.

Or his neck.

When he licked my cheek, I snapped. Fucking disgusting prick. I lost the giggling demeanor as quickly as if it had been wrenched from me when he slapped at my other breast. Moving sharply, I yanked away from him, twisting my body out of his hold. But either his grip or these damn knee-high boots caused me to trip.

It had to be one or the other because I certainly wouldn't admit drinking that much prior had been poor judgment, and the alcohol had affected my reflexes.

Demons don't make mistakes. We own them.

Mid-trip, before I had a chance to righten myself, he kicked my feet out from underneath me, and then he was on top of me, faster and heavier than I had anticipated.

Fuck.

"Get off me, you pig," I spat at him as he grabbed for my hands, unable to get a grip on my wrists as I beat at his arms and shoulders. He kneeled as he covered his face with his forearms, deflecting my blows. My attack wasn't graceful, but I didn't like being in such a vulnerable position unless I *chose* to be there. I was angry.

"That fucking hurts, you bitch."

But I kept hitting him, eventually curling my

fingers into fists and punching at every inch of him I could reach. I was pissed my little act hadn't gone to plan and I had been humiliated by this fucking human who managed to get me in such a defenseless position—on my back, on the floor.

"Steady there, gorgeous." The other voice was deep and vibrated through me as two large hands grabbed at my forearms, attempting to stop my onslaught of punches toward the biker on top of me. With the two men working together, they managed to get my arms above my head and pressed hard against the floor, tucked under the knees of his helper, and the larger man chuckled as the first started unbuttoning my too-tight leather pants.

He had the nerve to shush me as I growled, letting the sound pulse through me and fuel my anger. "Hush hush, calm down, lovely." When he leaned over me, I smelled beer and sweat. "Struggling will only make it worse when we take turns with you."

I bared my teeth at him, drawing another laugh from the rotten hole he called a mouth. There was something else I could smell, and in the split second it took me to recognize the scent, I pinpointed it with my senses and drew on it, allowing it to infect me. It didn't matter where the scent originated from, an old injury newly aggravated or someone simply accidentally cutting themselves, it tainted my senses, and enthused me.

Blood.

When I opened my eyes again, I had let them slide back into their natural glowing yellow, and it took the two men a second too long to see the change as I let my inner demon shift beneath the surface of my skin.

Leaping off me simultaneously, the first man screamed, "What the fuck?" as they both scrambled to their feet.

Crouching, I drew in deep, rattling breaths as I found the center between my human form and allowed my demon out to play.

Because I wanted to play.

Finding the center wasn't something I had mastered yet, and these men should pray I got the balance right.

Pushing myself to my feet, I launched across the room before he opened his mouth to cry out again, landing my forehead against his nose and snarling in delight as the blood burst forth—blood he couldn't wipe away due to my grip on his hands.

"Watch your hands there, buster," I growled loudly. "You just might lose them."

There was no chuckle this time, no snicker, only a whimper before he squealed like the pig he is when I twisted his hands, breaking the bones in his wrists and possibly some of the ones in his fingers as well. He dropped to the floor like a sack of shit the second I let him go, cradling his hands against his chest and sobbing.

First one down.

I turned to find the rest of the bar's occupants on their feet, and although they appeared weary of me, unable to draw their gaze from my glowing eyes, they were primed to attack.

I sneered. *Good.*

Not waiting for them to come to me, I charged at the closest asshole and grabbed his vest, using my weight and speed to lift him off his feet and slam him onto the floor. He was out easy. I hadn't planned it, but when the back of his skull collided with the hardwood, he was knocked out. Flicking my head up and sweeping hair from my face, I bared my teeth at the surrounding men, laughing when they backed off a step.

When I launched myself from the unconscious man, I leaped onto the next nearest, who immediately began screaming at a pitch I'm sure he'd deny later as I sunk my teeth into his cheek, then spitting in his face to get the fowl taste of his tainted blood from me before I swallowed any. A barstool was broken over my back, which, in itself, I could deal with, but then someone picked up the broken chair leg and drove it into my calf.

I won't lie—it hurt like a bitch.

Thank fuck for high pain tolerance.

Yanking the splintered wood from my leg, I turned the weapon against my attacker, returning the gesture and stabbing him where he had me.

He went down.

One of the women tried to break a bottle over my head, and my arm flew out on instinct. I caught her wrist before the bottle made contact with my skull. Her eyes widened, and she trembled under my grip, dropping the bottle which I caught with my spare hand, laughing again as this made her whimper.

She was pretty and shrunk under my gaze as I licked my lips, flicking my tongue over my teeth. I could take her, but I wasn't here for her. Not tonight. Although the ache in my pussy told me I'd need to deal with that aspect of my instinct soon, I wouldn't be acting on it now, not when I was having so much fun with my current projects. I leaned in close to her ear, purring at the way she trembled. I bet she shook the same way when she orgasmed.

"Run, bitch," I whispered.

She did.

In an attempt to use a move I had seen in a spy movie, while I failed to capture it with silver-screen grace, the next man went down with his head crushed between my thighs. By the time I had taken him out, the bar had emptied. The remaining men and women having fled, taking those injured and unconscious with them.

There wouldn't be a club for them to come back to.

Cracking open the bottle the woman had tried to

hit me with, I poured a portion over the wound on my leg. *Strange.* I frowned, unsure why it hadn't healed yet until I found a few stray splinters still embedded in my skin. Hissing between my teeth, I removed them and gave the wound another splash of bourbon. I could almost watch as the remaining gash closed up, then I poured the last of the amber liquid down my throat.

Tasted like shit but burned so nice.

I vaulted over the bar and set about pouring bottle after bottle onto the floor and tables and snatched up a stray pack of cigarettes on my way out. Using a lighter to light a cigarette, I then threw it over my shoulder into the bar. The flames crackled to life slowly at first, burning on the spilled alcohol before spreading to the wooden furniture and eventually licking up the walls. It didn't gain momentum as quickly as people seemed to think it did, but it also depended greatly on the bar's contents and could change from small fires to raging inferno in a second. I'd learned the hard way a few weeks ago when I had casually strolled out and had barely made it to the door before the flames reached a particularly volatile pile of kindling.

It singed my clothes, which pissed me off.

I liked that jacket.

As I sat across the street, smiling and watching the building burn, I only wished I'd grabbed

another bottle before leaving.
  A drink and a show would've been nice.

CHAPTER 3

ILSA

Whoever she was, this mystery redhead, she was a strange mixture of chaotic and organized. If she had a plan before she strolled into and decided to destroy these places, I couldn't find any evidence of it.

Yet, her error lay in her selection of locations. I'm no detective or private dick, but if television has taught me anything, it's to map out the locations and search for patterns. So, I did exactly that, starting in the most logical spot for me to get my head around this.

And fuck me, as I tracked her and my information increased, it was glaringly apparent she was moving in a fucking spiral. Not a perfect spiral, mind you, but there was a definite pattern there. I had no idea if she was even doing it consciously, but it hardly mattered. I spent an unreasonable amount of time on the internet and even more time wandering the area and asking questions of anyone who would talk to me. Not many were willing because let's face it, I looked like law enforcement. Relaxing my posture had done nothing. It was written all over my face—authority—and the locals in this area could see me coming a mile away. Now, I had reduced it down to three places for what I suspected her next targets could be, and three was certainly better than an entire city full of potentials—another biker clubhouse, a bar well known for the distribution of illegal substances well beyond the small-time exchange of a few tablets for a few hundred dollars, and a church.

I almost didn't choose the church, but she's a demon, after all, and I took my chances she'd want to destroy a religious icon. It made sense to me. As far as I knew, she hadn't crossed paths with a significant building of spiritual merit in her previous wanderings. They certainly weren't overly abundant down this end of the city, and maybe she'd be in the mood for some irony.

Or maybe they burned her flesh if she stepped foot on hallowed ground. I had no idea—this was all unknown territory for me.

The next issue was *when* she would strike because there was no clear pattern at all.

Sometimes there were only a few days between attacks but other times, weeks. Her means and method constantly changed, and this is why the authorities were skeptical these were the acts of one person.

Although she did seem to favor fire.

Irony.

One person couldn't *possibly* have done it alone because, of course, one person couldn't take out a room full of bikers, *surely.*

But they hadn't seen her move like I had—the way she twisted and flexed, discarding people to the side as though they weighed nothing.

It must be exhilarating to have that power. What I wouldn't have given to have some of her supernatural strength and mobility in my corner during my deployments.

Maybe then I'd have been fast enough to move out of the way of the shrapnel.

Squeezing my eyes shut, I subconsciously rubbed my leg where, underneath my cargo pants, the large scar now resided. It was a stupid thought to have, and I pushed it to the side.

No one could've protected me from the injury, least of all myself.

Maybe I even deserved it for the part I played in the situation.

Shrugging, my move now was to simply wander my suspected area in the evenings and hope I lucked out and was there when she was. It's not like I had anything better to do anyway. While I was quite capable of getting a job, I hadn't bothered, and I didn't need to with the funded retirement I was offered after the medical discharge. While I hated feeling as though I was somehow mooching off the system, nothing seemed worthy after what I had seen and done, the images of which still haunted my mind every time I closed my eyes. But this, potentially saving innocent people from a rogue being, *this* was worthy, and I was going to throw my all into it.

Perhaps if I could stop her, it would ease the feeling I was now a burden to the very society I had tried to help. Did anyone else see me the way I saw myself? Unlikely—with the exception of perhaps my family.

Did knowing that help? Not in the slightest.

So, I had wandered the streets at night and slept throughout the day, as much sleep as I could muster anyway. It didn't bother me. It felt good to have a mission again.

Humming absentmindedly, I kept my hands shoved in my pockets, the fingers of my right hand sliding up and down the handle of the silver knife I had picked up. One of the things I had learned while researching online—silver and salt—two basic things you could use to deter demons. Since I didn't fancy throwing a handful of salt at an enemy during a fight on the off chance I was completely wrong and she was simply a normal human, I had opted for a blade. A silver knife would stop humans *or* demons. I wasn't bad with a blade but preferred a handgun myself, or even better, a sniper, but a blade I could handle well enough to protect myself.

A lone woman walking the streets on this side of the city was a target, add to that the limp which I couldn't disguise no matter how hard I tried, and I might as well have had a flashing sign above my head saying *mug me.*

I wore my army pants, combat boots, and a tight black t-shirt to show that while one of my legs may have given up on me, my arms were still sculpted enough to fuck someone up. I simply hoped the ensemble coupled with the *get-fucked* expression I kept plastered on my face would be enough to deter any would-be attackers.

It worked.

Mostly.

A small group slowed as I approached them, and my shoulders tensed. I could tell they were going to be trouble before the sneers even crossed their lips as their eyes raked my body, lingering on my weak leg.

Shit.

One of the women grabbed my forearm as they passed, and I spun, twisting my arm from her grip and sliding the knife from my pocket in one smooth motion. The group laughed, an unsettling mixture of the high-pitched tingle of giggles and throaty chuckling.

"What's that? Your grandma's knife?" one of them sneered.

My eyes flickered to the silver blade. It wasn't designed for protection by any means, the handle and blade itself were carved with ornate patterns. It was probably designed to cut cheese or some shit. But any blade could do damage if you knew where to use it and what pressure to apply.

"Yeah, it's my grandma's, and it'd be a shame to sully it with your blood," I replied.

They were snickering again. But they weren't attacking, and I took that as a good sign. Perhaps they were weary enough of me to think the better of it. Maybe they realized anyone who would wander these streets alone—with a limp, carrying a cheese knife—had some serious shit going on, and perhaps they weren't the sort of person you wanted to antagonize.

Maybe they were all bark and no bite and were only showing off to each other.

Our little soiree was broken up when a gunshot rang out.

They all ducked, instinctively throwing themselves to the ground before pushing back to their feet just as hastily and bolting down the street.

Straightening, I listened. I guess my luck was changing.

If you consider almost getting shot lucky, then I was rolling in the pot of gold at the end of the proverbial rainbow, and not only because I was *almost* shot. But because of sheer willpower, by wandering the streets for weeks—the same four city blocks over and over again—I think I had finally stumbled across her next target at the right time.

Dumb luck wasn't how I liked to work, but it had saved my ass more than once before, so I guess I shouldn't question it so much.

Turning, I faced the bar across the street, the front of another biker clubhouse. It seemed incredibly ballsy to take on two such places in such a short period of time. Surely, they would be on high alert given the incident at the other clubhouse only a few weeks ago. But even so, I don't think they would be on the lookout for someone who looked like *her*.

The window shattered as another shot rang out, and I zigzagged across the road, dropped to my stomach and crawled the last few feet to the front door, still sitting ajar. Pushing it open with my fingertips, I slid my way up the outside wall, my back pressed against the bricks, and snuck a peek inside.

It was her.

Of course, it was.

Her eyes practically glowed with the glee adorning her face as she took down the biker with the gun, bending the metal barrel in her palm and laughing as he cried out in terror. There was nothing I could do to save the men in the room from her, and more than I probably should I was relying on her past pattern of not killing. But like clockwork, she didn't kill them. She only took them down one by one until the remaining fled, taking their fallen comrades with them.

Despite the detachment with which she attacked, as though her body moved on instinct alone, and the pleasure she seemed to take in the fight itself, I'd admit it only to myself it was impressive to watch. She moved with a strange grace, considering the violence of her actions, as though this was nothing but a dance to her, a playful flirt between her and her victims.

Cursing, I pressed my back flat against the bricks again. My eyes had been wandering over her body, taking in her curves, the pinch of her waist, everything down to the dimples on her cheeks.

I'd chosen partners poorly in the past, but checking out a *demon* was a new low even for me.

Why was I attracted to women who were bad for me? Did I crave the chaos? I had long ago accepted I couldn't control the world any more than I could control those who lived in it. Maybe by choosing partners who were bad news, who lived as though there was literally no tomorrow, I was hoping some of that freedom would rub off on me or perhaps I hoped they could stamp down the remaining need to control flaring inside me every now and then.

Yeah, I'd had a lot of time to think about this.

The need for freedom from my desire to control was a need that would never be fulfilled.

I had no control, but that didn't stop me from craving it.

I couldn't even control my own body anymore, forced to partially drag one leg almost uselessly behind me, a constant reminder I wasn't able to manage the situation enough to avoid or even see the explosion coming.

I hated it—the reminder, the truth, the reality of the situation—I hated it all.

So, when someone like her was about, not a care in the goddamn world, *being* the force of chaos that drives the rest of us mad when it interferes with the lives we've tried so hard to structure, I *hated it.*

It was almost like I hated her before I'd even met her.

Fuck, I didn't need to *meet* her.

This wasn't a date—she was a demon.

This was a mission.

Her attractiveness was literally not even a consideration.

Fuck.

Cursing again, I'm sure she saw me, a flash of yellow eyes and a grin before I had finished turning away from the door.

"Yeah, you better run!" she cried out. The vacant bar rang with her empty laughter—spoken *hah hah hahs*. I thought she was talking to me until the telltale sound of the last of the men stumbling out the back echoed through the bar. Waiting until the sound of their boots tripping over the broken pieces of tables and chairs subsided, then after a beat, I flung myself around and into the doorway.

And was met with one hell of an uppercut to the chin.

I went down, unable to maintain my balance. My ears were ringing, and spots of light burst in front of my eyes.

Fuck me! She's got an arm on her.

"Wait, you're not part of the club."

Blinking rapidly and trying to clear my head, I attempted to focus on her. Sitting upright, I was pushed back onto an elbow when she placed a heeled foot on my chest, the stiletto pinching painfully between my breasts.

She was smiling at me, not at all threatened by my presence, and something about that made me feel incredibly small. I was used to holding a certain level of intimidation about myself, but here she was, looking down at me as I lay on the floor, sticky with blood and alcohol, and her face showed only bemusement. I was in an incredibly vulnerable position.

And I was still noticing the shape of her goddamn legs.

Fuck!

"How do you know I'm not?" I spat at her.

She laughed again, a tingling sound that didn't suit her at all, and I couldn't tell if it was real. It was higher than I'd have thought. The sound I'd imagine coming from a petite blonde teenager, not the dark, sexy demon who destroyed buildings and souls.

Sexy? Aw hell. Now I know I'm in trouble when I consider someone who'd just flattened me with an uppercut sexy.

"Little Miss Army Boots, do you even need to ask?"

Her tone was derogatory but filled with humor, and I genuinely couldn't tell if she was poking fun at me or being playful like the whole world was a joke to her. In retrospect, it probably was. Trying unsuccessfully not to let my annoyance show, I knew the sneer had escaped my lips when amusement and interest flashed across her face before it was replaced with a devilish grin.

How appropriate.

"What's the matter, soldier? Don't want to talk about it?" Scowling, I resented the sing-song quality of her voice. When I didn't answer, she continued. "Whatever, I'm not here for you anyway."

"Why's that?"

She cocked an eyebrow at me, the smirk still plastered on her face. She wasn't letting me up but had slightly eased the pressure of her boot. "You don't belong here, you're not one of them, and it'll do me no good to take down some random bystander."

That answered absolutely no questions. *Do her no good?* What the hell did that even mean?

Glaring at her, I tried to keep her talking while I slowly slid my hand into my pocket.

"How do you fight in high heels?"

She pressed down against my chest, smirking as I grunted, angling her foot so the heel slipped between my cleavage and poked into my skin.

"I have a high tolerance for pain." She beamed.

"What about this, *demon*?"

Slipping the blade from my pocket, I lurched forward and slammed it into her upper thigh. She screamed and recoiled, leaving me to scramble to my feet as she staggered backward.

"*Silver?*" she cried. "What the *fuck?*"

I advanced as she retreated against the opposite wall, stumbling as blood oozed steadily from where the knife lay embedded in her thigh. "I know what you are, *demon...*" I said with a sneer, "... and this ends now."

Her eyes widened as she slid back against the wall, the patch of blood around the blade growing with each passing second. Tossing a glance at the wound, she'd then stared at me with an expression I couldn't read. She started groaning, and the loud rumbling moans filled me with a discomfort I couldn't explain. Everything about this woman loaded me with conflicting feelings, and I started to wonder if that's simply what demons did to people.

God, I was glad no one could hear my thoughts. I swear I sounded insane. I've so readily accepted this *demon* theory, there isn't any room left in my mind for the alternative.

Show me proof you're human or not, so I can maintain my sanity, please.

"Oh, ooh…" she whimpered, her head lolling from side to side, "You got me. I can't believe you stabbed me."

Frowning, I watched her.

Something wasn't right.

She staggered a few steps to either side, slapped her palms against the wall, and continued to wail with increasing volume. "Ooh, what a way to end. Who would've thought I'd be vanquished by a small brunette woman with a tiny dessert knife?" Sinking to her knees, she then shuffled toward me, and I backed away, shaking my head. Her hands were clamped under her chin, her eyes wide as she pleaded, "Please, have mercy. Ooh, I don't want to die. No please, *please!*"

Throwing a forearm across her forehead, she

looked at the ceiling, declaring loudly, "My only regret is that I never figured out what the fuck an elderberry is." With that, she collapsed backward onto the floor.

I stared as a muscle in my jaw twitched. "What the fuck was that?"

A grin lit her face at the same time she sat up. The way she moved sometimes gave me the chills—tilts of the head or sitting upright with a smooth motion and an arch of her back that defied what speed should be possible for such a movement. "Did you like my performance? I thought it was quite good myself."

"What's *wrong* with you?" I cried, my frustration and confusion bubbling inside.

Standing, she scoffed at me. "Oh, lighten up."

A shudder went up my spine at the subtle *slick* of the blade being pulled through flesh, and I wasn't able to stop myself from jumping slightly when it clattered as she tossed it to the side. Following its trail, my fingers twitched as it slid under the bar.

Dammit.

She approached me, those golden eyes flashing dangerously, and when I almost tripped over a fallen chair while backing away from her, her hand shot out and grabbed me, holding me up.

I had seen a lot, but the look in her eyes and the danger she radiated sent a shiver down my spine. My skin burned where she touched me, but not a burn I wanted to recoil from, a pleasant warmth making me ache for more. A flash reel of my previous partners ran through my mind. Yeah, I had chosen some incredibly poor partners in the past, but looking into her eyes, I knew she'd be the biggest mistake I could make. She was strong, fast, and capable—everything I used to be and was no longer. Beyond that, there was a physical attraction to her interfering with my judgment. I shouldn't be admiring her on any level. Not only was what she was doing wrong, but *she* was wrong.

And unnatural.

Demon.

My body was responding to her touch. That warmth flared under her fingers and singed me, sending a wave of fire through my body.

Gripping my arm, she gave it a slight squeeze, perhaps as a reminder of the power she held within her.

Maybe as a warning not to try stabbing her again.

I couldn't guarantee it.

Her eyes flashed again when she caught the defiance in mine. Hell, I shouldn't even be here. Why did I even think I could take her down? She was strength and grace, and obviously didn't play by the same rules as the rest of us.

No, I had to do *something*. I couldn't stomach the idea of innocent people being hurt. If someone was hurt, and I could've stopped it but instead chose to do nothing, it would make me equally to blame as the offending party. I don't think my heart could take it. So I had to try. I was right to come here, right to track her down. While I'd never forgive myself if I failed, I think I'd simply shut down completely if I had never tried at all.

Although her victims were hardly innocent themselves, the potential was always there for collateral damage.

Unacceptable.

I couldn't allow it and bared my teeth as I yanked my arm from her grip.

"Silver doesn't kill demons," she said, eyeing the patch of blood on her pants before mumbling, "Still hurts like a fucking bitch, though." Before I could take advantage of her momentary distraction, she grabbed my face, squeezing my cheeks together painfully. While she'd let my arm go when I shook her off, she hadn't shown the slightest bit of concern at touching me again. It was as though she knew she was stronger than me.

Dammit, *of course,* she knew she was stronger than me.

I was no threat to her.

She was so close, her hands hot against my skin, and she smelled amazing.

Where the fuck did that thought come from?

My legs weakened, and *fuck,* I wanted to lean into her touch, even though it was rough and painful. I understood now what that person online meant when they said *oozed sexual prowess*—it was in the air all around her. Incredible.

Her perfect lips curved as she grinned. "Am I turning you on? A happy side effect of being a demon." As she flicked her hair over her shoulder, the ends of it hit me in the face. I'm certain it was on purpose, and my anger flared, crushing down the throbbing sensation between my legs. "We're sexual beings, after all. Any other time, I'd take you to places you never dreamed of." I pulled a face, and she smirked. "Now," she said, turning my head until we were eye to eye, "How did you know what I was?"

"Your eyes."

She let my face go, stepped away from me, and paced the bar as I rubbed my cheeks. "That's fucking it? You saw my real eyes?"

"And your skin... it looked like black ink."

"How did you know it wasn't just your imagination?"

"I know what I saw."

Scoffing again, she placed her hands on her hips and studied me, but after the frown evaporated, she simply looked pleased. "Well, I must say, I'm impressed. Most people brush it off and assume they imagined it."

The anger bubbled in my stomach—at her, at my failure to stop her, and my naïveté in assuming something I read on the internet would actually help me stop a demon.

"You need to stop all this shit," I said, waving my arm at the broken remains of the furniture littering the bar. "Before someone innocent gets hurt."

Her face darkened, and in the time it took me to blink, she was in front of me again, her hand at my throat. "Who are you to say whose innocent?"

"Who are *you?*" I choked out, somehow finding the strength past my fear to raise an arm and press a finger to her chest. "Stop all this, now."

Her fingers tightened around my throat. "You know what I am, you should be more afraid. You think I can't feel the conflicting emotions in you? You think I can't sense you're battling arousal and fury?" My face flushed with embarrassment or anger, or possibly both, and she laughed again. "I can feel your pulse under my fingers. You know of my strength. I could puncture your skin, drink your blood… *drain* you."

I shuddered, yet something about her words flared warmth between my legs again. Her gaze shot down before back to my face. This was humiliating, and my body acted outside of the consent of my mind. She had said being turned-on in her presence was a side effect of her being a demon, but that didn't mean I had to like it. This resulted only in increasing my anger toward her. I was nothing more than a pathetic human, a bag of hormones that responded to her nature and instinct.

Earlier, I had thought I wouldn't want her to end up in the hands of those who wanted to kill her based on some flimsy evidence she had some level of integrity.

But now I had met her, she was simply infuriating.

Cheeky bitch. All that power and not a care in the fucking world.

Not hours ago, I had also questioned myself—why was I so ready to admit she wasn't human? The last thing humans needed was something else out there that couldn't be controlled or destroyed. Was I so desperate for purpose since my discharge I'd latch on to the flimsiest proof of a supernatural being?

No. I knew the truth.

There were memories, things I had seen and had told no one, things I now knew were true. Despite the force with which I had answered, *I know what I saw* when she had questioned me, the truth was I had seen it before, and like apparently many before me, I had dismissed it, telling myself it must have been my imagination. It must have been a trick of the light. It couldn't possibly have been real because eyes don't do that—eyes don't turn yellow.

But knowing what I know now, through research and my interactions with this woman—demon—

perhaps when I had seen those eyes change while deployed, it had been real. Because the more I considered it, the more it was so painfully obvious war was the perfect hiding place for demons.

So, when I saw her eyes the first time, I didn't question it because I had already spent too long questioning, and I knew myself better.

I know what I saw. Both times.

"Let me go," I hissed through clenched teeth, grabbing her wrist where her hand met my neck and snatching at her other arm.

She studied me for a moment longer. Her eyes flickered from my hands, resting firmly on hers before back to darting between my eyes. Slowly, she dropped her fingers from my neck, letting them graze my skin before she finally let me go.

We stared at each other for a beat, and she tilted her head. "Just stay out of my way," she said, and before I could respond, she had disappeared into the night.

CHAPTER
4

RAY

That army chick, man, she was something else.

Coming into my territory, into the part of the city I had claimed as my own, and telling me to stop having fun? Saying I might hurt an innocent person? Who the fuck did she think she was?

Innocence was subjective. People lived secret lives she had no idea about. Everyone had their surprises—I should know. I had spent my fair share of time in Hell working people's hidden truths from them, then torturing them with the knowledge of what they had done.

Or if they felt no guilt, simply using physical pain. That could be more fun.

But that woman, she had gotten to me. I felt the rage burning inside her as though my actions were a personal insult and how it counteracted the arousal she felt from being in my presence. It wasn't a lie. Demons do have that effect on humans, but we have to either consciously turn it on, or it can be a side effect when fueled by adrenaline. I'm sure all her anger couldn't have been directed at me, not really. No, she was holding rage for something or someone else. Yet she still insisted on protecting the society and people who had—judging by her limp and the worn-out uniform pants—done her no favors.

Grinning, I scrunched my wet hair between my fingers. Although, the look on her face when I had gotten close to her was something else entirely—her slightly widened eyes, the increase of her pulse, the hitch of her breath. She responded to me on every level and, more importantly, on the primal level that demons live and breathe in.

While demons had that effect on almost everyone, her response was something else—the way her body had craved to be near mine. Her mind had fought so gallantly against her body's betrayal. It wasn't *all* my instinct, she was attracted to me, and I mean, who wouldn't be? But the inner fight coupled with her anger, well, it was hard not to wonder what it would be like to fuck her.

Not by force, of course, but by seduction. A flick of my tongue in the right places, and I'm sure I could have her squirming under me. Maybe she'd be good with her mouth too.

Wrapping the towel around my body, I fell back on the couch, letting my legs dangle over the arm. It was nice to have a hot shower—scathing hot—stripping away the filth and sweat from the past few days.

It wasn't my shower, nor my home, not that it mattered. The owners of this place wouldn't be home for a few hours. I wasn't going to rob them, they had nothing of interest to me anyway. I simply wanted to have a shower and grab something to eat. Hardly a crime.

Perhaps this mystery woman would make things more interesting. It was starting to get a bit dull tearing places apart. Even the fire had lost some of its appeal. All those humans were the same—thought they were tougher than they actually were—and the few who had any fighting skills didn't last long enough for me to get the pleasure I needed from the brawl.

Typical.

Because I needed the rush from their pain in a fight and even craved some of the pain myself. Without it, I wouldn't be able to keep my demon controlled, and it would come out, much as it had begun to when my little army chick had witnessed the beginning of the change.

So, now someone was on to me and actively tracking me down? Very interesting. A game of cat and mouse I could play, luring her and then leaving her, driving her crazy.

Maybe then I'd take her. Make her so angry, fuel her with hatred, so when I finally got her naked, she'd be barely more than animal. I could find out what really drove the anger and lust that mingled so strongly within her body.

Added bonus—she was easy on the eyes. It was hard not to notice the curves of her breasts when I had my boot heel pressed to her chest, not to mention the lines of her neck when my fingers were around it. She was afraid of what I was—fair enough—most humans were scared of what they didn't understand. But she was strong enough to stand up to me, to seek me out, and that made her different.

Had she stabbed me in the leg instead of the chest because she didn't want to kill me? She obviously thought the silver would do more damage than it did. Or was the location of her attack purely for convenience?

I hadn't spent a huge amount of my time on Earth so far focusing on seducing humans, only enough to keep the side of my demon nature subdued sufficiently so I could focus on the other fun part of my nature—violence and bloodlust.

It was a strain sometimes not to kill.

But she, whoever *she* was, had intrigued me.

Unwrapping the towel and reveling in the sensation of the cool air on my body, I wandered my fingers down over my chest and stomach, dipping my hand between my legs. I was already wet. Of course, I was—always ready to go.

The tough façade she had—which I'm sure was only on the exterior—would crumble under my touch. I was certain of it. She posed something to me few other humans had—a challenge and a threat. Her fear of me had been an instinct, a gut reaction to what she knew about me, but beyond that was anger and a need to protect. I think I could have some fun with her.

I wish I knew her name.

Pushing two fingers inside my waiting wetness, I moaned loudly. I could tie her to the bed to be tortured with gentle touches and soft kisses, before driving her to the peak of pleasure over and over again, denying release, and simply watch her come closer to coming undone.

Before I watched her come.

She wouldn't be the type to simply lie there and take it, I could tell. She'd fight the binds to touch me the way I was touching her. She'd grab my hair and pull me to her when I pressed my lips between her legs. She'd be the type to grind against my face, and I bet she'd make the most delicious noises.

Touching myself, I came hard, not bothering to keep quiet.

But the orgasm had only left me wanting more. It had riled me up, and fueled my desire to take this woman, whoever she was. *My army chick.* To show her no matter how strong she thought she was, she was nothing, *nothing* compared to me. As a human, she was weak and susceptible. I didn't want to hurt her, simply show her *I* was in charge, here and everywhere.

And since I didn't want to hurt her—she'd done nothing wrong as far as I knew—the best way to show her I was in charge was to have her flat on her back on a mattress.

Or perhaps bent over, her face buried in the pillows.

Or on the floor, legs spread for me.

Shaking the image from my mind, I stood and stretched, leaving the towel to fall to the floor. Wandering into the bedroom, I scanned the closet. I did love my leather pants and boots, but judging by the rest of the apartment, their taste in clothes might be expensive, and you never knew what you might find.

Snatching a red blouse from a coat hanger, I shrugged it on, admiring in the full-length mirror how it hugged my body shape and played off perfectly with the tone of my hair. I hummed appreciatively to myself before going in search of a wallet or a stash of money.

Okay, so maybe I *was* going to rob them.

The question was, how had she figured out where I was going to be? Was it dumb luck, or had she tracked me somehow?

The next question was, how do I make sure I run into her again?

Striding out onto the street in my new outfit, I stood and sighed into the evening air, watching as the last of the sunlight disappeared behind the apartment buildings littering the street and into the distance. It was a bit of a stroll to get to where I needed to be, but I didn't mind. I might even encounter some fun along the way. I figured if someone started something with me, then that was fair game.

Generally, when I needed a rest, I came to the parts of the city bordering where the rich fucks and the poor bastards lived. They had better accommodations and saved me from walking too deep into the higher end of the city. Besides, *those* people had doormen, and I couldn't simply snap a lock to the foyer and get into the building.

As the night air settled around me, a shiver ran up my spine that had little to do with the temperature. I'd been pretty much doing whatever

I fancied since I got here, figuring that unleashing my inner desires for violence would keep my demon side at bay. But there was a complication. It seemed by doing whatever the fuck I wanted and containing control over my appearance only served to work up the side of me desperate to seduce into a frenzy. I'd like to think this was why I had such a strong reaction to army chick and the potential complication she posed.

But maybe it was simply basic instinct attraction.

She'd obviously seen some shit, been through the worst this world had to offer—perhaps she was a kindred being in that sense.

Maybe I was thinking about it too much rather than relying on instinct.

It wasn't long before I walked past the clubhouse I had been at the previous night. It looked empty. Apparently, the occupants had opted not to return. I had planned on burning it down until I was interrupted. Might as well do it tonight.

Perhaps I'd also see my mystery woman again, returning to the scene of the crime and all that.

Be predictable on purpose because apparently, I was predictable enough before for her to find me in the first place. Now I wanted to find her.

Grinning, the word *tease* flashed through my mind.

Tease her, play with her, fuck with her.
Fuck her.

Crossing the empty street, I was a little more than disappointed I hadn't encountered anyone along the way. I also kind of wished I had raided the liquor cabinet at the apartment.

Inside the bar, the door slammed loudly behind me as my boots crunched over the debris. I was busy pouring the remaining contents of the bar across the floor when someone cleared their throat behind me.

Smirking, I turned, bottles in hand.

"You seriously came back to finish the job? Didn't you think I'd be here too?"

Army chick crossed her arms over her chest and stared at me through the dim lighting. She wasn't overly tall, but I could see the definition of her arms, the tautness of her stomach. She was fit. I smiled at her, wide and genuine, before I dropped the bottles I was holding and noted the way she flinched at the sound.

That only made me grin wider. She stood her ground while I approached her, but I could feel the fear prickling her skin. Fear and anger and a dappling of arousal—a dangerous combination—as I pushed my chest forward.

I quite liked the scent of it.

Right before we were chest to chest, she dropped her hands to her pockets.

"Maybe I was hoping you'd come back and find me," I simpered, blowing cool air against her earlobe and making her shiver as I laughed quietly. "Why are you afraid of me?" I asked, taking a step back.

She cocked a dark eyebrow. "You're a demon."

"Yeah, but what did I ever do to you?" She frowned at me, evidently unsure how to answer the question. So I added, "What's your name?"

"Ilsa."

"I'm Ray."

"I'm not here to be your friend, Ray."

Closing the gap between us again, I slid an arm around her waist, splaying my fingers across the small of her back when she went to step away from me. "I just want to know what name to scream when I come."

She slashed at me with a blade, and I stumbled back, clutching at the bloodied gash running down my arm. My eyes flashed, and hers widened, and I knew mine had turned yellow for a moment when I had lost control of my anger. I was aroused by her presence, her closeness, and the way she seemed to simultaneously stiffen against me but also melt into my touch. Like her body was fighting her mind, telling her to give it up because it wanted mine.

Grasping a silver knife, evidently she had a stash of the things, her breathing was heavy as she watched me, looking as though she was ready to pounce or run but couldn't decide which.

"Silver again? What the fuck?" I sneered, wiping away at the blood and tutting at how it smeared against my new top. "I told you it doesn't kill me."

"No." It was her turn to smirk. "But it hurts like a bitch, right?"

Involuntarily my eyebrows raised. *Ballsy move.*

But she had pissed me off this time, and the anger wiped away any lingering arousal I had at her presence. Demons had two modes—fuck or fight—and Ilsa had just turned me from one to the other. Launching at her, she parried my attack with a shot straight to my nose, bent her fingers, and slammed the ball of her palm into my face. My head knocked back, and I tasted blood in the back of my throat.

Ilsa stared at me as I straightened. She was still in an attack stance, but her eyes widened as I growled. I was on her before she had a chance to react, tackled her to the floor and clasped my hands around her neck. She lashed out at me, swiping at my arms and face with the knife over and over again, each cut burning and searing my skin and sending a vibrant stinging pain through my being and stirring my demon. The wounds would heal, albeit not as fast as regular ones.

She ceased the relentless slashing only when I roared in frustration and removed a hand from her neck, snatching at her wrist and slamming her hand against the floor repeatedly until she dropped the knife. I'll give her credit where credit was due, it took a hell of a lot of force to get her to let go of the weapon.

She shouldn't test me. I could break her wrist as easily as snapping my fingers if I wanted to.

Ilsa was losing control of her composed exterior, her initial attack had been plotted, planned, and born, I'm sure, from training. But the mad slicing with a blade? That didn't seem like her style.

She was panicking.

These innocent people she talked about—didn't she realize she was one of them?

Doesn't she see I *could* have killed her during our last encounter, but I didn't? Isn't that enough for her to know I'm not out to hurt random humans? Apparently not, and I let my eyes slide into yellow when there was another spike of anger. The clarity of my vision increased as I stared at the woman between my thighs, her neck in my hands. She was bucking her hips against me, digging her nails into my arms.

Something crossed over her eyes, and her body language shifted. In one swift move, Ilsa wrapped her right leg around my waist and pulled hard on my right ear while her other hand grasped my face and her thumb pressed into a soft spot under my chin I didn't even know existed. My head was yanked to the side at the same time she bucked her hips, and using her leg, she maneuvered me off her.

Christ, I thought as I hit the floor. *What an overreaction.*

It's not like I was going to kill her. Only choke her until she passed out, and I could finish my work here in peace.

I made a mental note not to underestimate her again.

Once on top of me, she brought her hands between my arms and forced me to release my hold on her neck. The element of surprise sure helped, and I relinquished my hold on her. I dropped my arms to the floor and paused before calmly folding my hands behind my head. Above me, her chest heaved with every breath. I could almost see the adrenaline pumping through her veins and smell it in her blood. My pupils dilated with the thought of her life's blood and the idea of it on my tongue. I wondered what she'd taste like, if she would give me a greater high than other humans, and if I could absorb some of that anger and angst.

My relaxed pose seemed to disarm her, and she frowned. When she reached into her back pocket, I snatched at her arms, not in the mood for another assault with silver. The tingle of metal on metal sounded against my ear drums, and I laughed.

"Handcuffs? Oooh, baby," I cooed.

"I'm arresting you," Ilsa said as she brought her breathing into line and snapped one of the cuffs over my wrist. I let her, lifting my arms between us while she straddled me and allowed her to cuff the other wrist. The deepening frown etched on her forehead told me she knew my compliance was a trap, but she was still tied by some inner duty to do the right thing.

Sitting up, I brought my handcuffed wrists between us, my eyes flashing at the way hers widened at the closeness of our bodies. Fuck, she radiated such heat. Not only from the fight but simply her body pulsing so near to mine. I must have denied myself a fuck for too long because I wanted to take her so bad.

So, I did something crazy.

Crazy was kind of my calling card anyway.

CHAPTER
5

ILSA

It took me longer than it should have to realize Ray had snapped the chain on the handcuffs. I was trained, and while I'd come out of practice much faster than I thought I would, I certainly should've heard the telltale crack of a chain snapping. You didn't need to be a weapons expert to know that sound.

Especially since it occurred behind my head.

No, I heard it, but it just didn't register.

Because I was otherwise distracted.

While I was still on top of her, after she sat up and made some snide remark, she had *let* me handcuff her. I had seen what she could do, and while I bit the inside of my cheek, knowing this was a trap of some sort, I couldn't pass up the opportunity to cuff her on the off chance I read the situation wrong and maybe she felt remorse.

Yeah, right.

What exactly had been my plan? I wasn't sure. I didn't think I wanted to kill her, but I did want her to stop this mad reign she had taken up against the city. So, arresting and handing her to the authorities seemed right. They could deal with her then, and she wouldn't be my problem anymore.

Because somehow, Ray had become my problem.

But the sound of the chain snapping escaped my attention because after she had looped her arms over my shoulders, my adrenaline had peaked again when I thought she was going to strangle me. I had relaxed slightly around her, becoming lax when I normally wouldn't, definitely being more complacent than I should be in the presence of a demon. Lured into a false sense of security Ray wouldn't harm me because she had let me go before. But it was hard not to be fooled—coupled with the effect she apparently had on my hormonal and instinctual response—for whatever reason, I simply didn't feel unsafe around her.

Somehow, I knew Ray wouldn't hurt me.

Much.

I mean, she had tried to choke me.

The crack of the chain was lost amongst the adrenaline and arousal. Because in the same moment she had broken the chain as though it were made of cotton, she had pressed her lips to mine.

She fucking kissed me.

Ray didn't wait for me to kiss her back. Both my body and mind had decided working in tandem was no longer an option. She simply forced my lips apart with her tongue and took control of my mouth.

Ray tasted like cheap alcohol and fire as if the heat of her was going to ignite me. She was passion on long legs, and I swear my body had never responded to Kelly or any of the others the way it did to Ray. And *fuck*, that only served to make me fucking angry.

Anger which my body apparently channeled into arousal.

Because *Christ,* her lips were amazing.

Obviously, I had some fucking issues too because instead of pushing her away, I snaked my arms around her back and pulled her to me. I took back the power of the kiss and massaged her tongue with my own, flicked the tip over her teeth, and teased her with what I knew I was capable of.

And when she moaned.

Hell, if I wasn't sitting down...

Her forearm tightened around the back of my neck, and I clawed at her shoulders when what she was doing dawned on me.

Aw fuck.

She grinned against my lips as she pressed her other hand to my larynx, tightening until everything went black.

It was hot.

Too fucking hot.

Raising an arm, I shielded my face when I went to open my eyes and was met with an assault of light and heat. Then the smell of the smoke, dancing around the inside of my throat and into my lungs yanked me back into the waking world, and I sat up, clutching my head when pops of light danced before my eyes.

For a horrifying moment, panic gripped at my chest when I thought Ray had left me inside the building when she had set it alight. But I was on the street, the rough gravel of the road under my palms as I steadied myself, and the flames licked at the building through the now-shattered windows. The heat was unbearable even from this distance, and my eyes followed the pillar of smoke as it disappeared into the night sky. It wouldn't be long before the emergency services arrived. That, right there, being one hell of a smoke signal.

Despite the heat, Ray stood much closer to the flames than me.

With a sickening sensation in my stomach, I realized she was probably used to the heat.

I had been faced with my own mortality enough not to need a slap in the face of the existence of an afterlife. There are some things I didn't want to think about, and where I'd end up after I died, given all the things I had done, was one of them.

When I started coughing, Ray spun on her heel, and smiled wide when she looked at me. She came and sat next to me, yanking on my arm when I tried to move away from her.

"Sit, you need to rest for a moment."

"Why? Because you choked me until I was unconscious?"

She smirked. "Yeah, exactly."

We watched the building burn for a minute. Like the most fucked-up date ever. I wanted to do something, but what could I do? Turning, I studied Ray for a moment. She had a look that almost reflected tranquility on her face as she sat, mesmerized by the flames.

"Do you know why they call me Ray?" she asked without looking at me. I shook my head but didn't respond. When I didn't say anything, she turned to me, positively beaming. "Because I brighten your night," she said with a dramatic flail of her wrist toward the flame.

What.

The.

Fuck?

"Have you been waiting for me to ask so you

could tell your little lame joke?"

"Yes, but you're grumpy for some reason, so I had to set up the punchline myself."

"You choked me!"

"And you stabbed me, so I think we're even now. No?"

My eyes flickered to her wrists. "Where are the handcuffs?"

Ray nodded toward the building. "In there, do you want them back?"

"Funny."

"Oh, lighten up, Ilsa. What do you have to be so gloomy about?"

Losing my job, my livelihood, the part of me that made me feel worthy of a family that didn't otherwise accept me. Having my ass kicked by a demon. Being stupid enough to go after a demon in the first place. Then being aroused by said demon. Believing in demons at all. And finally, the injury that ruined my leg and career.

Glaring at her, I shook my head.

Then I heard it.

"What the fuck was that?" Ray asked. All humor was lost from her voice, and she sounded scared.

As I scrambled to my feet, my leg gave out underneath me, and slapping Ray's hand away when she went to grab my arm to help, I shushed her when she complained. Straining my ears again, I know what I heard, but I prayed I was wrong.

Screams.

"Ray, someone is in the building."

The adrenaline was surging in me again, and Ray took a step backward from the flames, shaking her head. "That's not possible, I checked and double-checked. There was no one in there."

Running toward the building, I recoiled when a supporting pillar collapsed, followed by a shower of sparks blasting through the front door. Scanning the area, I pivoted when the scream echoed out again.

Not this building, the one next to it.

The flames had spread.

"Help me," I cried, turning back to Ray. She hadn't moved, her eyes wide, still shaking her head. "Ray!" Clapping my hands gained her attention, then I pointed to the building behind me. "We have to save them."

Without checking to see if she was following, I raced to the adjoining building, shouldering the door until it gave way and immediately dropping to my knees. The place was full of smoke, blinding and choking. But through it, I could hear someone calling for help, and it drove me forward.

Removing my top, I wrapped it around my nose and mouth and squinted, constantly blinking against the blinding tears caused by the smoke.

"Where are you?" I called, moving the moment I heard a response.

Rushing past the front counter, ignoring the burn of my eyes as the smoke pummeled into my face with every step I took, I made my way to the back of the building.

A kitchen, ovens, large steel counters.

A bakery, some unfortunate soul had been here late, prepping for the next day.

When I found him, I cursed. With the collapse of the shared wall, an industrial oven had fallen, and his leg was trapped beneath it.

"Help me," he coughed out, trying desperately to prise himself free. I tried, God knows I tried, but the damn thing was too heavy. All too soon, I could see it in his eyes, the resignation, knowing he wouldn't get out of there alive. Cursing again, pain tore through my body as I tried once more in vain to shift the heavy equipment.

His eyes, I had seen that look, and I wasn't going to accept it. Not again.

But the oven wouldn't budge.

Ready to give up, I sunk to my knees. The smoke was overwhelming. If I didn't get out of this place soon, I'd die with this man. This isn't how I saw myself going out, but I couldn't bring myself to leave him.

I felt her presence before I saw her, and as Ray brushed past me, her face was clear as though the smoke didn't bother her at all. With a heave, she lifted the oven off the trapped man, and I scrambled to help him out from underneath. Looping our arms around each other's shoulders, we began to move out of the building, each limping on opposite legs.

Tutting, Ray came in front of us. I tried to scream at her to move, but smoke filled my mouth and lungs, and I began coughing again. Crouching, Ray lifted us each onto a shoulder and stomped out of the building acting like the only inconvenience to her wasn't the weight of two adults on her shoulders but the interruption to her night.

Carrying us across the street, she dropped us together onto the pathway against the building opposite. Ray and I held each other's gaze for a moment before she tilted her head, the approaching sirens her calling card to leave.

"I didn't want to kill anyone," Ray said, resignation heavy in her tone. She cast a sorrowful look at the man lying next to me, his injured leg, his face covered in ash and clothes burned, with eyes closed and breathing shallow.

When we locked eyes again, I frowned, trying to figure out what she was thinking. "Ray, you need to stop this."

She bit her lip, looking between me and the empty street behind her. I knew she would run, and there wasn't anything I could do to stop her. Saving this man's life trumped chasing her. Besides, she had proven herself hard to pin down when she didn't want to be, and I started to suspect I was out of my depth. Weren't there people trained to do this? Demon bounty hunters or something? Where do I even find them? My internet search history would look like that of a crazy person soon if I weren't careful.

Ray's eyes were shimmering, and with a pang, I realized she was holding back tears. Why did she care so much about killing? I couldn't wrap my head around it. My chest ached watching her fight through indecision like a child learning a harsh lesson.

All right, no bounty hunters then.

This was between her and me.

A different approach, perhaps?

I kept my voice quiet and gentle. "Ray—"

"Please," she said. "Just leave me be, will you?" And with that, she turned and disappeared into the night once again.

I couldn't get the look on her face out of my mind, not when the emergency services arrived, not when I indicated they needed to treat the man first, not when the police questioned me.

She was a demon.

So why should she care if she killed anyone?

CHAPTER 6

RAY

Telling her to stay away from me, I couldn't offer Ilsa the same courtesy.

A man had almost died, and it would've been my fault. What would I have done if Ilsa wasn't there? I froze on the spot. I had been so sure of my motivations, of my actions, and when she had warned me about potential collateral damage, I was able to brush the warnings off without a second thought.

Not once in my entire—and considerable—lifetime had I questioned myself.

But I was all shades of questioning right now, and I didn't like it. Not one little bit.

What the fuck was I even doing on Earth?

Was she right? I was no one to be deciding who was and wasn't innocent.

But I wasn't condemning anyone to death, I was simply setting back those who were doing the wrong thing—taking away their clubhouses, their labs, their places of dodgy business.

How could that be wrong?

A man had *almost* died.

But the key point was he *hadn't.*

But still, *she* had gotten into my head, this tough army chick. What was in this for her anyway? Some self-appointed vigilante. I liked her occupying my mind even less than I liked questioning myself. Because when I'd kissed her, it had been for several reasons. Distracting her, obviously, and secondly, because damn, why the fuck not? She was gorgeous and resisting me at every turn, and lastly, I just plain wanted to.

Tormenting people was what I did best. It was all I knew. And kissing her tortured her because she knew what I was and because it turned her on as much as it had me. I could feel her arousal when I touched her flaring up under my fingers.

Then it tormented her more because she didn't want to be turned on.

What I wasn't counting on was the distraction it would cause me. Because I let the kiss drag on longer than it needed to for the purpose I had initially instigated it. Because I let her take control of the kiss, and I liked the feel of her arms splayed on my back. She tasted amazing, and I wanted more.

Obviously, I should've given in to that part of my desires a lot sooner, allowing the people I seduced to fuck me or let me fuck them, then perhaps a single human wouldn't have infiltrated my thoughts so much.

But instead, here I was, creeping outside her apartment building.

She hadn't given me to the cops, which had only increased my curiosity about her. Why track me down, research me, handcuff me even with the threat of handing me in, only not to provide the information to the authorities when given a chance?

What was I to her?

There wasn't much to her apartment, and as I scaled the fire escape up the side of the building, I largely ignored the way it ground and creaked against the walls in protest to my speed until I was closer to her floor. Only then did I move with a little stealth, not wanting to alert her to my presence. This wasn't about confrontation but about me observing her.

Humans were at their most natural when they thought no one was watching.

Ilsa didn't seem the type who would like being watched, but my giving-a-fuck factor was pretty low about that. She stuck her nose into my business first.

Unable to see her, I pressed my nose against the

glass, trying to peer around the sides of the window into the other rooms. It wasn't a large apartment, but few around this area were. However, it was clean and tidy with everything in its place. A separate living area and kitchen already made it more spacious than many of the places I had seen, but it was sparsely furnished. I wondered how long she'd been here.

The window rattled in its frame with the force of her punch, and I almost toppled backward off the edge of the fire escape railing, clutching onto the ladder. Recovering my foothold, I glared at her through the glass. She had popped up in front of me, having been crouched on the floor under the windowsill. Rubbing her knuckles with her other hand, her eyes darkened as she watched me, lips pressed together in a thin line but not saying anything, not even showing satisfaction at being able to catch me off guard and making me jump. We simply looked at each other for a while before she unlocked and slid the window open.

As she slammed a hunting knife into the wooden windowsill, I stepped backward. She left the handle wobbling from the impact. Her message was clear.

My space.

"Hi," I said.

"Hi," she responded through gritted teeth. "Why are you here, Ray?"

"You intrigue me."

"That's great. Get away from my home, please."

"Nice of you to say please."

Her eyes narrowed, and she asked again, "Why are you here? I already lied to the cops against my better judgment."

"I never asked you to do that. I was wondering why you did."

Ilsa sighed, flicked the knife's handle, and sent it rocking again, the wood around the blade's point splintering slightly. "I don't know. You confused me. Why don't you kill people?"

"It's against the rules."

"What rules?"

"Our rules. I wouldn't last here long if I killed humans."

Her shoulders dropped, and she pursed her lips as though she was hoping for a different answer. I don't know what she wanted me to say, but I wasn't going to lie to Ilsa.

For some reason, it would feel wrong to lie to her.

"Is that the only reason? The rules?" Ilsa held my eye contact for a long moment. I felt like a child being scolded for some wrongdoing, and it took more willpower than I was willing to admit not to shuffle the toe of my boot against the grating and look at my feet.

"Look, Ilsa..." When I said her name, her eyes snapped to mine again, but this time I didn't look away. "I do what I want, playing out my nature as a demon, but I'm not going to kill innocent people either… that's not right. I may be a demon, but I know the difference between right and wrong, even if I choose to ignore it at times. These places I take down, those people deserve it, you know?"

"Be that as it may, it's not your call to make."

"Oh!" Crossing my arms across my chest, I pouted at her. "And whose call is it to make?"

"The authorities, the justice system. We have these systems in a place for a reason."

"Your justice system is more corrupt than me," I scoffed.

Ilsa didn't answer. I suspected I wasn't telling her anything she didn't already know. But for whatever reason, she wanted to believe in the system and that the law was right and good, even in cities like this.

It was no accident I had chosen this city, the sort of place where this type of destruction can go on without any real consequences. I mean, *shit,* it was so much more fun here than it was playing out my duties in Hell. I hadn't planned to stay for an extended period, but if I could act out my duties while on Earth *and* get to do whatever the fuck I wanted, why wouldn't I? Sometimes I wondered why more demons didn't come to live on Earth, and I supposed it was too much work. They'd have to figure out a way to sustain themselves, a place to sleep, food to eat, maybe even get a—I barely held my shudder down—*job.*

Shaking my head to clear my train of thought, I noticed Ilsa was still staring at me with an eyebrow cocked.

"Can I come in?" I didn't think her eyebrow could arch any higher until I asked that question, but there it was.

"What on earth for?"

I shrugged. "We could fuck?"

"I'm not going to fuck a demon." She looked as though she was about to laugh.

"You say that now." Testing the waters, I took a step closer to her. The look of amusement dropped from her face. "But you just wait."

"It's not going to happen, Ray," she protested, but her voice waivered when she got to saying my name.

"What's the end game here, Ilsa? Are we going to play this back and forth forever? You had the chance to turn me in, and you didn't, yet you've obviously been trying to stop me. What's your motivation?"

Ilsa opened and closed her mouth a few times, but no words came out. I noticed the way her fingers twitched toward the knife. I was asking questions she didn't know the answer to, or she didn't want to admit, and I felt the heat radiating from her with every step I took closer.

"Stop it," she whispered.

"Stop what?"

"The thing you do, your demon powers turning me on."

Grinning then, I bit my bottom lip. "I'm not doing anything, I promise you." Another step forward. "Any reaction you're having to me now, that's on you." The last step, barely a shuffle forward, any further, and I'd be tumbling through her window. "Maybe if you let me be *on you* too—"

I withdrew my hands just in time to avoid the window as she slammed it closed, flicking the lock. Smirking, I watched her as she glared at me through the glass. The glass wouldn't protect her if I wanted to get to her. I could break it as easily as if it weren't there.

I think she knew that.

But that was for another time.

If Ilsa wanted to play cat and mouse, I could play.

Maybe she wasn't used to being the mouse.

Blowing her a kiss, I vaulted over the railing and slid down the ladder.

CHAPTER
7

ILSA

Ray was lying. She had to be.

There was no other explanation for my reaction to her. It had to be those seductive demon powers she mentioned. It was the only reason it could be— the way the warmth rushed through my body with each step she took, that glint in her eye as though she knew exactly the effect she had on me, luring me to her with whatever powers it was demons held over humans.

By not turning her into the police, I had shown weakness, and now Ray would exploit it for everything it was worth.

But the way my cheeks had flamed and the warmth had flushed between my legs, I didn't trust myself to stop her from making a move if it came down to her and me again.

Pressing my back against the cool glass of the window, I slid to the floor, so I was once again hidden from sight in case Ray decided she was going to play another spy game on me.

Ray was good, I had to admit that. I almost didn't see her tailing me home. She flitted in and out of the darkness as though she belonged there, and I supposed she did.

Beyond that, she had asked the very question I had been grappling with these past few hours.

Why didn't I turn her in?

I had been following her for weeks after months of researching her moves and patterns. *Hell*, I even had an ex-girlfriend break the law by providing me with copies of forensic reports so I could track this *demon* down. Then when it came down to it, I hadn't made the move. I hadn't told the police officers what I knew about where she was likely to strike next, her apparent motivations, or her name and what she looked like.

Nothing.

Simply opting to tell them I had been in the right place at the right time to save the man in the bakery.

The man we'd rescued had eyed me while I recounted my version of events, and although I knew he remembered Ray being there, he didn't say anything. That was one thing about this city, there was so much corruption the citizens tended to stick together. I imagine he assumed if I were lying about being alone, then I had a damn good reason for it.

Or I was into some fucked-up shit, in which case, he was best to keep his mouth shut as well.

I could tell myself it was because I knew the police wouldn't believe me, but that was a cop-out because I didn't have to tell them she was a demon but simply provide all the other information and let them do their jobs.

But there was one point that was sticking in my head—the look in Ray's eyes when she thought she had condemned an innocent man to death.

It was fear that cut her to the core. To me, this seemed beyond the fear of breaking whatever rules were laid out for her and her species. I couldn't even begin to delve into that Pandora's Box right now. This was something else. Somewhere inside her, she cared for people, and beyond that, she genuinely believed she had been doing the right thing.

I'm not a religious person, I never was, but compassion and empathy aren't words I'd associate with demons.

So here was a woman who intrigued me as she claimed I did the same to her. She was strong, physically, of course, but had such a badass attitude to life, it was almost contagious to be in her presence. I felt I had to pile on the tough exterior to be worthy of her company. Those fucking eyes alone could melt me, she was beautiful all right. Ray was funny and cheeky, she was playful—and then there was the real kicker—she had empathy and compassion somewhere beneath all the other shit. So, all this was wrapped up in a bad-girl package that fits right in with my type.

Except, she was a *fucking demon*.

What the hell was wrong with me?

RAY

Sitting across the street, knees curled up to my chest and arms wrapped around my legs, I watched Ilsa's apartment building.

What the hell was wrong with me?

Why did I care what she thought about me? She had taken all the fun from my pursuits, and now I was at a loss as to where to go. I had it all figured out and had been doing nothing but enjoying my time on Earth. But now, now I was second-guessing everything.

All because of her.

I wanted her.

I wanted to take her and punish her for what she had done to me—complicating my mind with her human imperfections when I had the perfect plan. Her body under mine, writhing with pleasure, there was only enough pain to make the pleasure all that more delicious.

Fuck it.

There was no way I would stop what I was doing, not now. Standing and straightening, I stretched my arms toward the sky and groaned loudly. My muscles ached. I needed a hot shower or a sauna. Anywhere hot and humid so my muscles could relax. But first, I needed to work out the tension that was thick within my body. She'd gotten in my head.

What was it they said? Go big or go home.

There was a venue I had been avoiding as it seemed too big to take on. It wasn't hard to notice the steady stream of unruly characters that hung around there—groups of people that went down the alleyway and didn't come back for hours. The door was almost hidden, and I was impressed. The outline hard to feel even when I ran my fingers straight across it. Push, release. Simple but effective.

Whatever was going on back there, they didn't want it to be found.

Of everyone who could've found it, I did.

But they're going to wish the cops had found it first.

CHAPTER
8

RAY

It was on the news this time. Apparently, the one I had taken down last night was big enough even the cops couldn't keep it out of the headlines.

Look at me. I was famous. No photos, please.

They assumed it was gang wars, one gang trying to hone into the territory of another. Next, they said we could expect shootings in the area as this escalated. People were no longer safe on the streets as though they had ever been in this area. The cover story that the fire had been an accident was immediately quashed by the leaked security camera footage of the injured and limping gang members escaping out the back minutes before the building went up.

It was chaos.

And it reignited my passion for the game.

Fuck Ilsa, she can do what she wants. If she wants to continue the cat-and-mouse game, then so be it. I had no issue with that, but I wasn't going to stop what I was doing and give up on a good thing because she couldn't keep her nose out of my business.

What did she care about potential collateral damage anyway? She didn't know these people, and it made no difference to her at all. I'd make every assurance the wrong people didn't get hurt, and whatever her issue was beyond that was none of my concern.

So, taste for the chaos reignited. I didn't wait weeks or even days before striking again but moved on to the next venue only a block away the very next night.

Sure, I could've done the damage during the day, but there was something so much more invigorating about the night, and let's be honest, the worst people came out to play in the darkness.

This time, a mechanics shop.

Which was more like a chop shop.

Too many cars went in and didn't come back out again, not the same color or with the same identification number anyway. You show me someone in this area who drives a Mercedes, and I'll accept this place is legitimate, and there's nothing sinister going on behind the scenes.

Besides, what mechanic is open well past

midnight, the lights glowing across the otherwise empty street, the sounds of buzzsaws and drills blasting through the silence and mingling with the sounds of bass from the nightclub down the street?

"Hello, boys." I sauntered into the place after breaking the lock on the roller door and forced it up, the resulting crash echoed in the silence following my entry.

When they simply continued to stare at me, I felt the impact of my entrance wasn't being appreciated.

"I said..." I cleared my throat, dropping one hip and placing a hand on my waist. "*Hello, boys.*"

"Get out of here, lady," one of them snarled, wiping his forehead with the back of his hand and leaving a smear of grease.

"Well, that's no way to treat, as you say, a *lady.*" Smiling, I crossed my arms. "So, which one of you is in charge?"

"What do you want?"

I turned, eyeing the man who had questioned me, holding a heavy wrench and was resting it in his palm. "I want the biggest, strongest guy here, so when I kick his ass, you'll all know I mean business, and you'll leave the building so I can burn it down."

The laughter that rang out wasn't unexpected, and I continued to smile brightly at them, letting my eyes flick around the room, taking count as more of them emerged from corners and shadows. I saw him before he had moved in front of the others. He was hard to miss, slightly under seven feet tall and large arms crossed over his barrel-like chest.

"Are you the boss?"

He sneered. "No, I'm the one you have to get through to get to the boss."

Laughter again.

I cracked my knuckles, fully entering the garage. "All right, let's get this out of the way."

He was still laughing when my fist connected with his jaw. Anyone else it would've knocked them on their ass, but for this monster truck of a man, he simply stumbled back a few steps. The laughter ceased, and it was my turn to giggle. He cracked his knuckles this time, sounding with several fewer cracks than it had when I had made the move. Ducking as he swung a punch at me, I flitted around him and connected another to his kidney, forcing a grunt from him.

With every move, he was becoming angrier, and the jeers from the audience that had formed did nothing to keep his rage under control. The grin didn't fall from my face, even when he connected with my jaw, and although I had moved so his knuckles barely scraped it, it was still enough to send me stumbling back.

Soon, the back and forth was boring me. This slow-moving man who relied on sheer power rather than skill was bothering me, and I found myself yearning for the heat of the fire.

Time to clear these fuckers out.

With a cry, I ran at him, littering his body with a smattering of punches from his groin up his torso, and when he bent as he was winded, I grabbed the back of his head and punched his face, over and over until he lost consciousness. He was a heavy bastard, so I let him drop to his knees and then forward onto his face when he was no longer holding up his weight.

Stretching my elbows behind my back, I clicked my tongue against my cheek. "All right, who's up next?"

Apparently, it was the man with the wrench, and he kept the weapon at bay as he approached me.

That was a mistake.

Because as soon as I got it from him—followed by the snap of one of his fingers breaking with the force of my assault—it only took one hit from the wrench to take him down. Apparently, after this, they tired of my shit. Several of them pulled out guns, and I wondered why it took them so long. I took two shots to the leg, the bullets going clean through, but when I kept coming for them was when there was real fear in their eyes that I could take them down before their minds cleared enough for them to retaliate.

The rest followed shortly afterward, coming at me. Those who decided they were better off not fighting and valued their own asses more than saving the building assisted in dragging out their unconscious or unable-to-walk comrades.

Throwing one of them across the room was fun, first slamming him into a table and running him along the length as his head collided with every item on the surface before I propelled him from the edge.

Like in the movies.

When the last of them was clearing out, I spun on my heel as I felt someone standing behind me.

"Aw fuck, seriously?" I groaned.

"Hi, Ray."

Ilsa stood at the entrance, her eyes firmly ignoring the destruction littered around me—the tools, floor, and cars splattered with blood—and staring only at me. She looked disappointed, and for the life of me, I couldn't figure out why. Did she seriously expect me to stop because we had a short conversation?

"Apart from the fact you want to fuck me, why are you here?" I asked.

"You need to stop this. I thought you learned."

"You thought wrong. I'm not killing anybody, so just stay out of this."

"No."

"Listen," I approached her, and while she flinched, she stood her ground, one hand in her pocket touching what I'm sure was another silver knife. How many of those fucking things did she have? "You can't control me, and you don't seem to genuinely want to kill me. So, either take me down or leave me alone."

She said nothing. I had hit a nerve.

"Ray, these people, they aren't going to take this forever. They might come after you."

"But—"

Screaming, I dropped to my knees and fell forward. Reaching behind me, I was desperate to remove the metal stake that had been plunged into my lower back.

"Ray!"

Concern in her voice?

What the fuck?

Some pain, even for me, was hard to ignore, and I felt my skin surging and shifting as my demon filled with rage at the attack. Snarling, my shoulder blades cracked and shifted as I bent my arm back, twisting my elbow on a third joint that didn't exist in humans, and managed to grab the stake. It was slippery with my blood, and my hand kept sliding away as I tried to remove it.

I needed it gone, so I could heal. It was steel, and the wound would take care of itself in a matter of minutes if I could only get the fucking thing out.

Turning at the sounds of struggle, I watched as Ilsa forced the man who attacked me to his knees, her arm wrapped around his neck from behind in a chokehold and his fingers scrambling uselessly against her arm as he weakened. When he stopped fighting, she gave him another shake to be sure he was unconscious before rushing to my side.

Ilsa, so composed and well-trained, was flapping about as though she had never seen a wound before. I could read her. She wasn't hesitating because she didn't know how to deal with the wound, she was battling internally because she didn't know if she wanted to save me. Or if she *should*.

"Stop thinking about this. You've already taken a man down to help me." At my words, she cast a glance at the unconscious man on the floor, her eyes wide. "Just help me, I can't reach it."

"We need to get you to a hospital," she said.

"No hospital," I forced the words through gritted teeth. "Just get this fucking thing out of me."

With both hands and a better grip, she was able to slide the stake from me. The suction sound of flesh as the wound sealed while it was removed had my shoulders slumping with relief. Hearing it clank as it hit the ground, Ilsa moved around until she was kneeling in front of me, her hands hovering around as though she was afraid to touch me. My shoulders were rolling, the muscles begging to turn into my demon form, but I kept it under control.

Barely.

Twitching, I waited a moment, and she simply

watched me.

When the wound had healed, I raised my eyes to hers. She was frowning, but when she saw my expression clearly, she stood and took a step away from me. Did she think I'd attack her after she helped me?

Bit of a fucked-up opinion of me, but okay, I get it. I was a demon, after all.

"You helped me," I said, pushing myself to my feet.

"Yeah."

"Why?"

"I'm... I'm not really sure. He attacked you when your back was turned."

I smirked. "Well, yeah, but I had just beat the fuck out of their entire boy band. I kind of deserved it."

She was rubbing her arm. "Probably."

"So, this brings me back to the same question. Why?"

"I don't know, all right? Fuck," she muttered. "Look, I've done you a favor now so can you just stop all this shit already?"

She was so odd.

"Why do you care so much?"

Continuing to rub her arm, she still stared hard at me, although I could tell she wanted to look away. "Look, I kind of get why you're doing what you're doing, but I still don't think it's your call to make. I think it would be better if you just stopped."

"If you want to protect those who are innocent, why aren't you helping me?"

Ilsa glared at me. "Because there's a right and a wrong way, and whatever the justice system may be, there are still good cops out there. I can turn these places in, and they can take them down the right way."

"Oh, please, you think the cops don't know these places are here?"

I was hitting her with a lot of uncomfortable questions. I knew that, but she needed to face the truth—her system was corrupt and useless, and *my* system was, well, corrupt too, but also very effective. Her conscience was holding her back, some misguided view of right and wrong and how the world should work even though, especially here, it very clearly didn't work like that anymore.

I'm not sure it ever did. History has been littered with people doing the wrong thing, people from all walks of life, and in all careers and levels of power. I'd know, since I came across many of them when they reached my world.

My methods may not stop them, may not be the answer to single-handedly bringing crime down in the city, but it sure as hell would slow them down.

"Ilsa..." I kept my voice gentle as I approached her like she was an animal that might spook. "This has been fun, but you don't need to keep playing this game with me." She opened her mouth to answer, but no words came out. "If you miss me, you can keep showing up at these places, and we can do this again, but otherwise, I think you need to accept you're clearly not going to do anything one way or the other and just back off."

Anger flared in her eyes, followed by a tiny flicker of doubt. "Stop doing what you're doing, Ray, or I'll give the cops the info I have on you."

It was hard not to smile. "That's hardly a threat to me, and you know that." She lifted a shoulder, and I spoke before she had a chance, "Chose a side, Ilsa. Either you want to stop me, or you don't. While I love messing with you, even I'll lose interest in this game eventually."

"You seem to have some level of compassion, and for that reason, I don't want to see you die. I feel like you're a misguided missile, pointing your energies in the wrong direction."

"So..." I said, closing the gap between us and reveling in her sharp intake of breath, "... you better stay out of my way then."

ILSA

"Do you want to wash your hands before I burn this place down?"

Snapped out of my thoughts, I looked at my palms, slick with Ray's blood from removing the steel stake from her body. I never got used to the feel of blood on my hands and rubbing my fingers together, I never wanted to be the sort of person who did get used to it. I'd seen my fair share of it, probably more than my fair share, but people who were in professions that dealt with it day in and day out—doctors and paramedics and nurses—Christ, I don't think I'd have it in me.

Sometimes the sniper was easier.

Part of me wanted to tell Ray not to burn this place down, but there was another part of me lingering underneath and occasionally reminding me it was there. The feeling had a name—resignation. I couldn't stop her from burning this place down any more than I could stop innocent people from being killed, or that I could convince myself every time I pulled the trigger it would be the one that made a difference and saved the world.

Mostly it saved a handful of people and mostly that was enough.

Searching her face, she was watching me intently, trying to figure out the inner workings of my mind by simply staring. What was Ray to me? I was starting to fear she simply represented something beyond what she physically was. Maybe to me she was an embodiment of destructive forces that took innocent lives with them as they went.

Except this time, I had fooled myself into thinking I could stop them.

Without her, I'd have to find something else to focus on.

"Yeah," I muttered. "Let me wash up."

My thoughts continued to wander as I followed her between the cars, stepping over tools and small pools of blood. When we found a bathroom, she turned the tap on over the sink, and I shoved my hands under the blast of icy water.

After a beat, Ray said, "Hey, army chick, surely you've seen blood before?"

I stood there, staring blankly at my hands while the water rushed around my fingers, making no attempt to get soap or even rub them together, simply letting the water run from red to pink. Still lost in my thought, being dragged back and forth from one conclusion to the next, every one left me lost and not knowing which direction to take.

"Here," she said, shoved me to the side, and stood in front of the sink before grabbing my hands and washing them under the flowing water.

"I don't need you to—" But she shushed me, lathering up the soap and working it between my fingers and over my wrists.

"When I'm done here, wanna get a drink?" Ray asked.

Giggling when I stared at her, she simply shrugged and continued washing my hands before turning the tap off and snatching up a paper towel to dry them. Taking it from her, I finished drying myself. I'd already let her get too close.

"How about we go for a drink *without* you burning this place down?"

Grinning at me, she waved a finger in my face. "You can't control me that easy. The fire is my favorite part."

"I would've thought the beating up the bad guys was your favorite part?"

"They're all my favorite parts." She smirked. "So, how about that drink?"

"Maybe another time."

"Wanna fuck?"

"You keep suggesting that like it's going to happen."

Ray bit her lip and raised her eyebrows at me. "That's not a no."

"No, Ray."

"Aw, you're no fun."

This wasn't news to me.

"Are you like this with everyone?" I asked her.

Pausing, she tilted her head. "Nope, only you."

"Why?"

"I like your stubbornness and your morals and loyalty even though they're misguided. And there's something so fun about fucking with you."

"Thanks," I pushed the word out through gritted teeth.

She giggled. "You're welcome."

"Let's go." When I turned to leave, she grabbed

my arm and spun me around, frowning now.

"Ilsa, I'm going to burn this place down, okay?"

"No, that's not okay. Why can't you just leave it be?"

"I'm doing good things here. Why can't you see that?"

"You so conveniently forget the man in the bakery."

"Oh, *please*, that was *one* time." Arching an eyebrow at her, I waited. It can't have been the only time there were close calls with innocent bystanders.

"Okay, fine," Ray added. "Maybe like three or four times, but no one has ever died!"

"He almost did."

"He didn't, though."

"Ray—"

"Ilsa, *fuck!* Make up your mind, will you? Either you want to stop me, or you don't. Either you want to talk to me, or you don't. You can't have it both ways because you and I both know I'm not going to stop simply because you keep showing up and asking me nicely." Ray grabbed my shoulders and shook me. I should've stopped her, but she was right, and I hated it. "What do you want?"

Purpose.

I was jealous of her, of her purpose, of her mission, of her ability to undertake it without fear.

"Let me go."

She did, and I took a step back. The rage burned within me, starting in my gut and working its way up my chest until my breaths were heaving. I could see the anger in her eyes reflecting mine. I was disrupting her, ruining her game because I wasn't playing my role in it. But I had no role because I had no end game here. I kept showing up to stop her hoping the answer would present itself to me, but things never got any clearer. Either I'd have to kill this woman, this demon, or leave her be.

"Just fucking stop this shit, Ray!" I yelled. She raised her brows but simply crossed her arms over her chest, dropping a hip and looking at me impatiently. Storming out, I slammed the bathroom door behind me.

But I wasn't angry at her.

I was angry at myself.

CHAPTER
9

ILSA

"Oh, you have *got* to be fucking kidding me."

Standing at my front door, her arm was outstretched as she leaned heavily on the door frame, that cocky-ass grin plastered on her face. I was about to tell her where to shove it, but then I gave her a better look over, forcing myself to shift past my initial reaction of having her at my doorstep—anger and confusion—and giving way to something I tried not to do too often to those who may not deserve it—compassion. The kind of compassion that goes beyond duty and makes my chest ache.

But seeing her now… *fuck.*

How I was going to explain to the landlord about the trail of blood leading from the elevator to my front door? I had no idea. The trail ended at her feet as she stood trembling, her grin having dropped a moment after I had opened the door. Blood was dripping from wounds on her exposed midriff, her taut stomach smudged with handprints as she had tried to stem the flow.

With as much of her weight as possible leaning on her arm, which shook with the effort of holding herself up, she simply nodded slightly and looked at the floor as though she already knew what I was thinking. Even though her clothes were black, as they mostly were, the thick, sticky patches of blood were still visible across her chest and legs. The rattling of her unsteady breathing was unnerving.

"Jesus, Ray, what the fuck happened?" I whispered.

In what I imagined was a huge effort, judging by the grimace painfully stuck on her face, Ray raised her head. When she made eye contact, I sucked in a breath, as I always did, despite our differences—a mild way of putting it—I wasn't blind to how beautiful she was.

And those golden eyes, well, they were hard to ignore.

Eyes that usually blazed with passion and fury were now filled with pain, and if I didn't know Ray better, I'd have sworn she was about to cry. Her deep crimson hair lay limp around her face, streaked with blood. Seeing her like this struck pain in my chest which was hard to ignore. I had tried to hurt her before, then helped her for reasons I still don't understand. But now, watching one of the strongest beings I had ever encountered, weakened and trembling, noting the lack of the cheeky flare from her eyes, well, it tore at even my own heartstrings.

"Please," she whispered, her voice cracking. "I didn't know where else to go."

I caught her as she passed out.

Why is it that although I had been trying to stop her myself, learning her habits and working my way into her life so she couldn't take a step without me knowing about it, that I suddenly cared she was hurt?

Because it wasn't done by me?

Because I felt some claim over her now?

Because I hadn't solved the enigma which was this demon woman?

What hit me the hardest was the realization I didn't want to see her suffer. That somewhere along the line, we had forged some fucked-up bond where we fought and disappeared without any real intention to do anything about it. Like a hero and a villain from a comic book, we needed each other as much as we hated each other.

The hatred seemed to be mostly on my behalf, I'll admit. Ray had continued going about her merry way while I had battled my conscience every damn step of the way.

Hatred mixed with desire was a difficult combination to deal with, so I expressed it in the only way I knew how.

Anger.

There was a time not too long ago when I thought I knew how to kill a demon. It turns out, I didn't know shit. But what I could tell you was the silver bullets used by whoever had attacked Ray wasn't one of them. Although they would hurt like hell—pun not intended—from what I had gathered, she couldn't heal until the foreign body—the silver—was removed.

Until then, she was in agony, bleeding openly and in and out of consciousness.

Which was apparently where I came in.

"I bet you're loving this." She forced the words through gritted teeth as I dug into another wound on her torso with tweezers, searching for the remaining silver fragments.

"I'm not, actually."

"Come on, Ilsa, admit you're enjoying it, even a little bit."

Ray howled as I yanked another bullet from her

torso, dropping it on the kitchen counter. I had her lying on the breakfast bar, pulling my stool up close and doing the best I could not to miss anything in the poor fluorescent lighting and the beam of the torch from my toolbox.

My lips twitched, and I knew she saw it.

"I knew it," she whispered, a hint of pride and a chuckle in her tone before lying flat again. Her forehead was covered in sweat, the moisture mingling with the blood in her hair. I wondered if that was hers or someone else's but didn't want to ask until I was sure I was ready for the answer.

"Looks like I pissed off the wrong person this time," she said, seconds before snarling at me, her eyes flashing when I pulled another bullet from her leg. "Fuck!" She hissed. "You could at least try to be gentle."

I arched an eyebrow at her and again said nothing.

Why had she come to me?

I didn't know where else to go.

That made sense. It's not like she was going around making friends.

"I know what you're thinking," she muttered.

"Sure you do."

Ray scoffed. "Please, you're easy to read. At least for me."

"You talk an awful lot for someone getting bullets removed."

She flinched. "You're thinking…" she jolted again, and I slapped her leg to keep her still, "… did the person who shot me intend to wound me, knowing the silver wouldn't kill me, or were they under the impression as you were that the silver would destroy me?"

"Was it an attempt on your life or a warning?" I muttered.

"Right."

I didn't give my answer straight away, but I certainly had my suspicions. "Maybe you've been stepping on the wrong toes."

She scoffed again but said nothing.

By the time the final bullet was removed, and I had done a suitable amount of digging around to search for leftover fragments, her body was covered in a thin sheen of sweat, and her face was pale, making her golden eyes and red hair stand out even more than they usually did. I'm guessing she was in more pain than she'd like to admit, and I hated the part of me that felt bad about that fact. She'd caused more than this amount of pain to others—maybe demons weren't immune to karma.

Slapping a gauze pad, harder than necessary, on her thigh, she sat up abruptly and snarled at me, baring her teeth as it turned into a hiss. It took all my willpower not to recoil from her. When her eyes flashed yellow like that, and she exposed her teeth—all I could see was the demon in her.

I had saved her.

Surely, she wouldn't attack me now in my own home.

Surely.

She flexed her fingers before rubbing her legs lightly, hissing when her hands passed over the wounds.

"Maybe you need to reconsider what you're doing," I said.

She glared at me before the glare melted into a smile.

"Demons..." she started, and paused before continuing, "... are supposed to do whatever the fuck they want. No pissy little attack is going to stop me from doing just that."

"That pissy little attack would've knocked you out for good if I hadn't have patched you up."

"And yet..." she held her arms open, a muscle in her jaw twitching as a shot of pain moved through her with the motion, "... you did, and here I am."

I glanced at the floor, unable to hold her gaze any longer. Ray had done nothing but eat up my thoughts since the moment I first saw her. First, as a demon existing in this world, then as an enemy to be stopped before becoming someone who filled me with conflicting thoughts and feelings that tortured me into the night.

"Why do you do it, Ray? All these things?"

The question felt different here, in my home,

than when I had asked her at the scenes of her crimes. I still couldn't quite look at her. Every time I did, it flared a need inside me I wasn't comfortable with. Not only because of the things she had done but what she was. Somehow, I had accepted she was still a living, breathing being—a being with emotions, thoughts, and a personality which both filled me with rage and made me smirk when I thought of her when I was alone. But I couldn't accept my lust for her. I much preferred it when I felt only anger and my desire was simply to stop her.

Ray slid her legs off the table's edge, so they were dangling in front of me. She had taken her pants off so I could deal with her wounds, the clothing too tight to roll up the leather. I tried not to look at where the black lace of her panties met her skin. I was fighting a losing battle.

"I am what I am, Ilsa. I need the chaos, the destruction to fight and fuck, and all that good stuff that drives me on an instinctual level. If I don't, I'll lose control of my demon."

My brow furrowed. She talked about the demon as though it were a separate part of her, or maybe it was simply separate from the human form she took on here on Earth.

"I follow the rules of being on Earth," she continued. "I don't kill... no innocents get hurt."

When I huffed, she paused. We were both

remembering the man in the bakery.

She was a whirlwind, this woman, revealing layers upon layers of complication and conflicts I didn't imagine when I first suspected her true nature. I wanted to know why she was here, what she was hoping to achieve, and if she had any dreams—things I'd wonder about other people, other humans. But she wasn't other people, she wasn't even of this Earth, this plane of existence. She had lived a life of inflicting pain and torture, but obviously, there was some cosmic cycle here beyond my understanding.

When I finally raised my eyes to hers, the look she gave me, like she was going to eat me alive, pulled a whimper from me. Her gaze shot to my lips and back up to my eyes, and she smiled a dangerous smile. I had so many questions for her. In the beginning, I had only wanted to stop her, but now, now I wanted to know everything. What was it really like for her in her home, and why she wanted to be here instead? My feelings toward her were still mostly hostile—*mostly*—and I hadn't fully relaxed since she came into my home, despite her weakened state. I didn't trust her, what she was or what she was capable of, and I still wanted her to stop this ridiculous mission she had set for herself.

Before someone innocent got hurt.

Before she got herself killed.

Because for whatever reason, Ray felt she was

doing the right thing, and I guess in some fucked-up way, she was. But I stand by my loyalties, and these actions were not hers to make. Being a vigilante wasn't the answer to the issues that plagued our society and world.

"Ray..." I started.

She moved fast.

My hands hovered by my sides, too shocked to respond as she leaped from the counter and straddled me, assaulting my mouth with hers and forcing my lips to open with her tongue and teeth. Her hands pushed desperately through my hair, combing it back with her fingers as she dominated my mouth. Ray's hands moved swiftly along my body, and my head was spinning as she fondled my breasts with expert fingers, flicking at my nipples through the fabric. I wished I had put on a bra, or at least something other than my flimsy nightshirt before I opened the door.

But then again, as she pinched my nipples between her fingers and thumbs, giggling against my lips as I groaned, I'm glad I didn't because it would simply have been a barrier to the sensations vibrating through me.

When she pulled away, I kept my eyes closed, reveling in her taste.

Whiskey and cigarettes and lipstick.

All things sinful.

"You little tease." She laughed. "I knew you never

really hated me."

And with that, she lifted herself from my lap and strode toward the front door, snatching up her pants from the couch along the way. When she turned back to face me, her eyes were blazing gold against the fire of her hair. As I stared at her, my jaw dropped, and I was barely able to process what the fuck just happened.

"Um…" she actually had the audacity to look uncomfortable for a moment, "… thanks for fixing me up." Then the grin was back. "You taste good, gorgeous. We should do this again sometime without the bullets."

As the door closed behind her and the shock wore off, the rage began to build again in my gut.

CHAPTER 10

ILSA

It's usually me. I'm the one to walk out after anything intimate. But having it done to me? That wasn't sitting well, grating against me like nails on a chalkboard as I stayed exactly as she had left me, too stunned to move for several minutes.

Still tasting her on my tongue.

What the hell did Ray think she was doing? Simply proving a point she held some power over me? That the entire time I wasn't a threat to her?

In the beginning, I wanted to take her down. Hell, I had every intention of it. I had literally stabbed her. The realization the silver was nothing but a painful inconvenience to her only served to solidify my resolve she shouldn't be here and needed to be stopped.

So, why had her fear of killing someone innocent

shaken me so much?

Ray had exposed herself to me, a part of her that cared for the innocent, as bizarre as that seems for a demon. Too often I had seen the other side of the coin—people who viewed collateral damage as a necessity to war, casualties which, while unfortunate, couldn't be avoided because there was a *bigger picture* to consider. They didn't see it as another human life lost, as a person with parents, perhaps children, and someone who loved them.

Then there was this *demon*, displaying more humanity than I had seen from a lot of people.

It didn't make any sense.

After Ray left, my body fought me, and I couldn't get back to sleep, spending a restless night tossing and turning in bed before giving up and curling up on the floor. A habit I had tried to work myself out of since coming back, but sometimes the unforgiving floor felt more like home than a mattress ever could.

On the floor, I had managed to sleep through most of the day. My sleep pattern was all fucked-up anyway from too long of sleeping through the daytime and going out at night demon hunting. Because apparently, that's a thing I did now.

Hours of broken slumber were interrupted by thoughts of yellow eyes with black slits for pupils, bright red hair, and lips to match. The nightmares haunted my sleep until the images slipped into recent memories of flesh on flesh, lips on skin, fingers on her, and of wanting to be in her. I had tried to shift Ray's face from my mind, replace it with Kelly's or Alex's, or any other number of women I had been with.

But I couldn't.

She was a force within me now.

And I hated her for it.

Deciding I needed to dunk my head in a bucket of coffee, and not the shit I kept in the apartment, but actual proper coffee, I dressed without showering and began to wander down the street in the fading light of late afternoon to a local café I had decided to call my regular. The barista was a young man who always looked like he had a world of questions to ask about my injury or my story, but he never did, and I respected that. But he'd hold the door open for me as I left, and whether he was doing it because I was a veteran, because of my injury, because I'm a woman, or simply because he was being nice, I wasn't sure. But whatever the case, the gesture didn't go unappreciated.

On my way back, I hadn't even had a chance to sip the brown gold in the cup when someone said, "Tell her to back the fuck off."

I spun on my heel, shifting my stance immediately into defensive. As I had passed an alleyway, a man had stepped out and into the light. Quickly, I did a double-take of the street—it was empty. He was talking to me, but why?

"What?" I responded, letting the aggression slide in my tone. Keep them on no uncertain terms—I'm not afraid of you, and I can protect myself.

"Tell her…" he approached in three swift steps, grabbing my wrists when I went to step back from him, the hot coffee I had planned on throwing in his face falling to the ground, "… to back. The. Fuck. Off."

"I don't know what you're talking about." I continued to try to pry his grip from my wrists, using all the weak points I could think of, but he wouldn't budge, and it was starting to get painful.

"That fucking demon bitch is more trouble than she's worth, and if she doesn't stop, she's going to find herself in a worse place than Hell."

I froze. Was this the person who had shot her? Why was he confronting *me?*

"I don't know what you want, but I've got nothing to do with her, so let me go."

When another, equally as tall man came up behind me, my attempts to move into a more defensive pose was hindered by the first man's grip on me. I'm capable, but even I'd have collapsed to the ground after the two punches to my kidneys were it not for the strength of the man still holding me up by my wrists. Gritting my teeth against crying out, I kneed the first man in the groin before flinging my head back and catching the other in the nose with the back of my skull.

While the crunch of the cartilage was audible, the second man simply laughed a deep and dangerous sound that sent a chill up my spine.

The man in front grunted, his knees bending, but he didn't let me go.

His eyes flashed yellow.

Oh shit.

There was nothing I could do as I was forced to my knees, the second man kicking behind my legs and the first pushing down until I was on the ground between them, arms stretched up with my wrists still firmly clasped in his hands.

"Please, I don't know what you're talking about." I kept my voice as steady as possible.

Not steady enough.

Screaming wasn't me and wasn't something I did often—in fact, I can't remember the last time I screamed. But after he shifted both my hands into one of his and slapped me hard enough my ears rang, fear crept up my spine, tickling the back of my throat in a need to release it. Because these men weren't really men, and I had no idea if they held themselves to the same rules Ray had talked about.

Worse, they seemed to think I was involved in what she was doing, and apparently, I was about to pay the price for her sins.

"We're going to leave you with a message for her…" the second man said, leaning in next to my ear and tickling his fingers down my ribs, "… and I'd remember the message if I were you. Because next time, it'll be worse, and you'll be naked."

As they dragged me into the alleyway, I screamed before a hand was slapped over my mouth.

Part of me kind of wished the silver *had* killed Ray before things got this complicated and I started feeling empathy for a demon.

Because look where it had gotten me.

I hobbled my way back to my apartment, without the coffee I had set out to get, but with a series of cuts and bruises I didn't seek. Fuck, I ached, my muscles screaming in protest with every step. I'd had worse, and I'd recover from this. A good long bath and maybe another bout of ill-advised drinking and some painkillers, and I'd get through it. I never wanted to rely on alcohol to pass through pain, physical or otherwise. But the humiliation of this entire situation was beginning to pile on my shoulders.

How could I have gotten myself so badly tangled in this damn situation? Whoever Ray had pissed off obviously thought I was involved somehow, and now I was dragged down into her shit.

Footsteps came running up behind me, and I hissed through my teeth as my training took over. I ignored the pain, dropping into a defensive stance and pressing my back against the warm bricks of the building behind me, hands raised and ready to strike.

"Ilsa, what the fuck?" Ray trotted up to me as I dropped my hands, my shoulders slumping as my guard was dropped and exhaustion took over. Her eyes raked over my body, and when she lifted a tentative hand to touch the bruises and blood on my face, I slapped her hand away. I didn't need the sympathy in her expression nor any of her help. None of this would've happened if it weren't for Ray and my weakness toward her.

"Don't touch me. Just get the fuck away from me!"

Ray backed off, only half a step, and I hated that I cared about the confusion and pain in her eyes. Up until now, this whole back and forth with us had been nothing more than a game to her. But this wasn't a game anymore. It never really was, and she needed to understand her actions had consequences.

"This is *your fault,* Ray!" I felt close to tears, and I let them burn against the back of my eyes and throat, refusing to allow them to surface but using the anger they fueled. There was no way I was going to let her know how much she had gotten to me. Dragging me into her bullshit and not having to deal with the fallout.

"My fault? How?"

When I pushed myself from the wall, I stumbled slightly as I moved toward her and angrily shook off her hands as she reached out to steady me when my limp got the better of me in my weakened state. Pressing a fingertip into her chest, I glared at her. "They think I'm with you... they came for *me.* They wanted me to tell *you* to back the fuck off because you're obviously pissing off the wrong people."

"Ilsa—"

"Don't say anything, Ray, just stay away from me. Stop doing whatever you're doing because it's getting out of hand now. People are getting hurt. *I'm* hurt."

Moving to turn away from her, she gripped my arms, regret flashing across her face when I hissed again as she aggravated my already aching muscles. My back and shoulder blades were grazed from the gravel of the alleyway as I tried to fight the men off, knowing I had no chance but having to fight anyway. Cleaning those wounds was going to be a barrel of laughs.

"Ilsa, let me make things right," she said.

"How do you propose you're going to do that?" I scoffed out.

"Firstly, I'm going to take care of you as you did

me. Secondly, we're going to stick together until we find whoever did this."

"Why should I have to stick around while you sort out *your* mess?"

"Because they obviously already think we're together. Do you really think being alone is a good idea?"

Pressing my lips together, I glared at her. I know she noticed the way my shoulders slumped and how I leaned my weight ever so slightly against her grip, trying hard not to, but with every passing second, my body screamed louder at me to stop. Because I needed to rest, and I knew she was strong enough to hold me.

Because I wasn't afraid of her anymore, and she could keep me safe.

I hated I found comfort in that.

Ray was right about sticking together, and I hated that even more.

What the fuck had I gotten myself into? I simply wanted to protect this neighborhood, even those who didn't necessarily deserve protection. Apparently, even that comes at a cost, no good deed and all that.

"What are you proposing?" I asked, grinding my teeth together against both the physical pain and embarrassment of this whole fucking situation.

"We'll stay at your place. We'll work together, and then when it's over, if you don't want to, you'll never see me again."

"Why my place?"

She bit her bottom lip, but there was a sparkle in her eye. "I don't have a place. I just kind of move around. We're instinctual beings. I need sleep, I lie down. I need food, I eat. I'm not fussy."

"So you can sleep on the floor then," I said.

"I don't even qualify for the couch? That's rough."

"House rules. Humans on the bed, dogs on the couch, demons on the floor."

It took all my remaining strength not to shudder at the way she looked at me, her bright teeth on display with the grin and a dangerous glint in her eye. "We'll see."

CHAPTER 11

RAY

Knocking out a steady rhythm on the door, I could keep this up all night. Given the choice, I'd put my stamina to better use, but I was also very easily entertained, even knocking out a few tunes with both hands to break the monotony like the fucking genius maestro I am.

Tat tat tat, tat tat tat tat, tat tat, tat tat tat.

"I can do this allllll night," I sang through the door. "In fact, I might add some singing to the mix since you're enjoying my percussion so much. Here we go—"

As I sucked in a breath to belt out something I'm certain would've been, at the very least, as majestic as squawking can get, Ilsa opened the bathroom door.

Christ, if looks could kill, I'd fall dead where I stood.

Her expression was icy as she tightened the towel around her body. "What. Do. You. Want?" she pushed out through gritted teeth.

I couldn't help it. I smiled. There was something so incredibly amusing about annoying her. I mean, I found it entertaining to bother most beings, humans and demons alike. But Ilsa, there was this delicious push and pull between us. A lingering attraction was right under the surface, and for her, the attraction was buried beneath a few layers of anger and denial.

Understandable.

I've never been around a human who knew what I was before, and there was something incredibly invigorating about it.

Besides, Ilsa had let me go more than once, then she had *not* turned me in when she could have, and actually helped *and* looked after me when I was injured. So whatever it was she was battling within herself, whatever lies she was telling herself to get through the days, she was fighting a losing battle. I wanted to keep pushing her buttons until she came apart, then maybe she'd talk to me properly.

"You need to let me clean your wounds," I said.

"Ray, I'm not going to let you bathe me."

"I didn't mean—"

"Please, just let me have a bath. Then I'll come

out, and you can annoy me all you want, okay?"

Pouting, I stepped back as she closed the door, thankful she at least didn't slam it in my face but instead pushed it closed with a gentle, but all the same, final click. I'll take it as a sign maybe she recognized there was care behind my offer to look after her, and it wasn't fueled purely by my desire to have her naked.

It seemed only right with all she had done for me, considering she obviously wasn't my biggest fan. I told her I knew the difference between right and wrong.

Perhaps I was a test of *her* morals, and it bothered her.

It wouldn't be the first time I tested someone's morals.

Striding across the room, I slumped onto the couch, unzipped my boots, and tossed them to the side followed by my socks, and wiggled my toes as I threw my feet on the coffee table.

Might as well make myself comfortable.

When Ilsa stepped out of the bathroom, I must admit she looked better. She was moving with a bit more ease, although I'm sure she was still in pain. I'd like to say she looked relaxed, but she walked with an edge to her posture, and when she sat on the opposite end of the couch, her back was stiff.

"What's the plan?" she asked before holding up a finger when I went to answer. "Tomorrow. Whatever we're doing, we'll start tomorrow. I'm exhausted, and I just want to relax."

"Yeah, you look real relaxed." If at all possible, her spine straightened even more at my comment, and I smirked. "I'm not going to hurt you."

"I know," she said hastily before she took a deep breath, almost forcing herself to loosen her posture. Her body slumped, and she leaned back against the couch, muttering again, "I know."

I waited a beat to see if she had anything else to say and cleared my throat before grinning. "I figure we find out who tried to kill me and had you beat up, then take them down."

"That simple, huh?"

"I don't see why not."

She arched a dark eyebrow at me. "Because whoever they are, they're obviously well-connected." I'd have sworn for a moment there was a hint of amusement in her face, but it was gone as soon as I had seen it. "And you managed to piss them off. I don't think it's going to be as easy as walking in there and *taking them down.*"

"You want a plan?"

Ilsa smirked then, briefly, but it was there. "You say it like it's such an unreasonable thing."

I slid across the couch closer to her. She didn't flinch or move away, but her back stiffened again. "Maybe we should just wing it."

"All right."

It took a certain amount of willpower not to do a comical doubletake. "I expected more of a fight," I said.

"I'm too tired to fight with you. Actually, I think I'm going to go back to bed."

Staring at her until she started to shift uncomfortably under my gaze, my face dropped. "But... it's so early."

She looked at me how I imagined a teacher might at a complaining child. "What do you want me to do, Ray? Do you want to watch movies and play truth or dare in our jammies?"

"I dunno." It was my turn to shift around in my seat. "We could stay up."

"And do what?"

Fixing her with a stare, I purred, "I'm sure we'll think of something."

She flushed, then chuckled, then went silent before releasing a heavy sigh, a matinee of the emotions that ran through her. "Ray, why did you kiss me?"

Shrugging, I said, "I was horny."

"Is that the only reason?"

I wasn't sure what she expected, so I told her the truth. "You're hot, and you intrigue me. Maybe I wanted to bang."

"Really, *bang* is the term you use?" Ilsa almost laughed again. This time it was so clear that she was trying to stop it. She *hated* the part of herself that relaxed around me and talked to me like an equal, but she kept betraying herself.

I did finger guns, the gesture immediately feeling unnatural. Too late now, I had to roll with it. "Pow pow!"

Ilsa stared at me. I should've kept my mouth shut.

Then she laughed, and while it was filled with nervous energy, I still loved the way it sounded, rolling off her tongue as her eyes squinted slightly, dimples in her cheeks I couldn't have noticed before they made themselves known when she smiled. Damn, she was cute *and* sexy.

"Good night, Ray," Ilsa said. "Don't rob me."

Her bed was cold—the hidden space between the sheets filled with the chill of the night. But once I passed through no man's land and slid closer to her sleeping form, her warmth captivated me again.

Ilsa was on her side, curled up on the very edge of the mattress. She grumbled when I placed a hand on her shoulder, rolling her onto her back.

Without opening her eyes, she muttered, sleep heavy in her voice, "What are you doing?"

Hushing her, I lowered my lips to her ear. "Just go with it."

When I pressed my lips to hers, her eyes shot open, and she mumbled my name against my mouth. I don't think my name has ever sounded better. Her hands found my shoulders, but she didn't push me away. Instead, she lingered for a moment, her fingers twitching with the physical manifestation of her indecision. But as I leaned over her and pressed my tongue into her hot, waiting mouth, she gripped my shoulders and pulled me closer to her. I thought she was going to protest when I kissed my way down her neck, but instead, only a guttural moan escaped. She didn't even argue when I pulled her tank top over her head but simply complied and lifted her arms so I could toss it to the side.

This wasn't a time for questioning, and I think Ilsa knew that. This was simply a time for pleasure. There were many complications outside this room, but not now, not tonight. She was mine to claim, and I would lay that claim.

Ilsa had worked her way into my life, and I

wanted her.

What I wanted, I got.

She was so warm, her skin burned under my touch as I ran a hand over her breast, squeezing gently before pinching her nipple. Kissing her again as she moaned, I smirked at the way her hips moved, lifting from the mattress and gyrating, desperate to find mine. I had to remind myself to be gentle. I had waited too long to give in to this side of me, focusing more on the lust for blood and violence, and my demon craved the meeting of the two.

Sex and power, pleasure and pain.

But Ilsa didn't need that. She needed to be taken, needed the pleasure but not too rough.

Not this time.

Ilsa needed to trust me.

Shifting over until our legs were intertwined, I lay on top of her, already naked. She gasped when she found this out for herself, running her hands down my back and stopping barely short of touching my ass, searching for panties that weren't there.

"You were so sure of yourself, weren't you?" she whispered against my shoulder as I kissed her neck. I could feel her smile against my skin, and I giggled.

"I keep telling you, I can read you like a book."

"Ray..."

But she said nothing further, and I lifted a leg,

pressing my thigh against her warmth and running my teeth over her throat, licking up her cheek and biting gently at her earlobe. She was grinding against my thigh, hard, desperate for the friction, and I chuckled again.

Lifting her arms over her head, I guided her to wrap her fingers around the frame of the headboard.

"Don't let go, soldier."

There was something in her eyes, a flash of defiance. I had struck a nerve referring to her as soldier. It didn't surprise me she harbored some traumatic memories, but there was something else there. A rebellion against higher ranks, perhaps? I grinned. It would be an interesting thread to pull to see what lay underneath.

I couldn't help it, tormenting humans was second nature to me.

Ilsa cringed slightly as I licked her cheek, and I giggled before pressing my tongue into her mouth again. I felt her arms relax as her grip on the headboard slackened, and I broke the kiss, slapping gently at her wrists.

"I said don't let go. Don't make me spank you."

Her eyes flashed, this time with lust, and smiling, I knew.

She *wanted* me.

Pressing her breasts together, I licked between them before moving down, dipping my tongue into her belly button and making her squirm again. Kneeling at the edge of the mattress, I bent at the hips, inhaling deeply as her scent intoxicated me when she spread her legs for me. She was so wet already I could see her pretty pussy glistening even in the room's dull light. Tucking my hands under her ass, I hooked her legs over my shoulders and buried my face between her thighs, lapping hungrily at her pussy. I wanted to taste all of her, and after spending some time licking and sucking on her clit, reveling in the delectable moans and praises spilling from her lips, I buried my tongue inside her, the mound of her hair tickling my nose pleasantly.

Fuck, she tasted so fucking good. She was practically dripping around my tongue.

Pursing my lips, I sucked on her clit again, rolling the sensitive bud around my tongue before repeating the motion. Ilsa was coming undone, and glancing up over her stunning body, I took in her hands, still gripping the headboard like a good girl. But her knuckles whitened as she started grinding against my face, desperation fighting her control. Taking a finger, I pushed it inside her, moaning at how easily she took the penetration, so wet and ready. Finding her G-spot, I rubbed it in tandem with my attentions on her clit, and her cries reached a new pitch.

She was close, and I was going to bring her there.

Fuck, Ilsa was gorgeous, writhing on the bed like that, teetering on the edge of letting go. It almost seemed as though she were holding herself back like she didn't want to allow herself the pleasure of releasing with me.

She'd have no choice in the matter.

"You better come, Ilsa…" I mumbled against her inner thigh, leaving a trail of playful bites in my wake, "… because I'm not going to stop until you do."

She moaned again and shuddered when I doubled my attention on her already sensitive clit and added a second finger inside her.

Ilsa came with a warm flush around my fingers as I continued to lick and suck at her clit, pushing her past her limit until she was trying to squirm away from my touch. Removing my fingers, I gripped onto her hips with both hands, barely controlling my strength as I held her against her struggles. I pinned her to the bed and sucked hard on her clit as it throbbed through her orgasm. She was stronger than I thought she'd be, and I'm sure my fingers were digging painfully into her as I fought to hold her still.

"Ray, *fuck!*" she cried out. The break in her voice ignited something within me, and I growled against her skin. As my demon gained control, I realized how foolish it had been to wait so long between sessions of fucking because I kept going, drawing out her orgasm until she grabbed a pillow and slammed it over her face to muffle her screams.

I kept going.

"Ray..." Ilsa panted, grabbed at my hair, and tried to push me away from her heat. "Stop, please, stop. I can't take it—" Her fingers tangled in my hair as another wave of pleasure gripped her, and she cried out again.

She could take it, and she would. Because I wouldn't stop until I'd had enough of her taste and her orgasms built one on top of the other. Her legs began to spasm, and her grip on my hair was painful.

When I pulled away, wiping my face on the back of my hands, Ilsa collapsed back against the mattress, her chest heaving. She was practically whimpering, and I was loving every second of it, loving every sound of submission trickling from her perfect mouth.

Crawling over her, Ilsa automatically placed her hands on my thighs as I straddled her lap again and sat atop her.

"Ilsa," I said.

She still had her eyes closed, her leg twitching intermittently under me. But I didn't have the patience for her to recover, not with the way my instinct raged through my veins at the taste of her. She was delectable, coming undone underneath me like I knew she would. Ilsa was strength and submission, and she didn't put up with any shit. She was everything I needed to balance me out.

And she was fucking hot on top of that.

I shook the human thoughts of distraction that served no purpose for me at this moment from my head. Leaning forward, I bit into her neck, and she cried out, rage edging on her tone as she gripped my shoulders.

Straightening, I grinned at the way she glared at me, rubbing at her neck.

"Sit up," I commanded.

She paused, too long for my liking, and I leaned forward again, this time flicking my tongue over her nipple before biting into the flesh of her breast.

"Ray!"

"I said, sit!"

Her frustration matched mine, and I could hear it edging in her voice. But I was bordering on losing control, and I didn't have time to care about her feelings. Pushing herself up on her elbows, I lifted myself from her only enough for her to sit, leaning her back against the headboard. Her hands came to rest on my hips again, and I began grinding against her, chasing friction for my release.

"You can't be mad at me," I whispered, blowing the words against her ear and loving the way she shuddered. "You let go of the headboard when I told you not to. You're lucky I'm not spanking you right now."

There was that look in her eyes again, both daring me against it and inviting me to do exactly that. But that would need to wait for another time. If I were to take her like that now, I wouldn't have the control I needed not to hurt her, and she might never let me touch her again.

Right now, I couldn't imagine being in a world where I wasn't allowed to touch her.

"Touch me," I let my voice soften, darken, and drip with seduction as her eyes became heavy with desire again.

She was soft and gentle, running her hands from my shoulders over my collarbone and finally to my breasts, palming them with open hands. Gripping her, pushing my fingers on top of hers, I forced her to grab at me, and her eyes met mine as she understood. She can't hurt me, so she can do as she pleases. Harder than she has to anyone before. I needed it, liked it.

The sound of her slapping my ass reverberated around the room, and when I lifted my lip in a snarl, she smiled sweetly at me, raising a brow as though in a challenge. Before I could protest, she spanked me again, and this time an involuntary growl escaped my lips.

The pain was so sweet.

"You're treading dangerous territory, soldier," I snapped.

But I couldn't continue my protest because her

hand that wasn't gripping my ass had snaked between us, between my thighs, and she was rubbing the ball of her palm against my clit. I groaned and ground myself into her hand, needing this more than I realized.

"More…" I whispered, hating how weak and mild my voice was but unable to do anything about it.

She slipped two fingers inside me, and then a third, and I cried out, gripping her shoulders.

"Ride my fingers," she said, watching my face as I took in the feel of her fingers inside me.

I began bouncing on her hand, using her fingers for my pleasure. When she shifted so her thumb was rubbing against my clit, I moaned as she gripped my hip, pumping her fingers in and out in time with my movements.

"Ray—"

Dropping down, I closed my mouth over hers, swallowing whatever she was about to say. This wasn't time to talk, and I groaned into her mouth as I licked her tongue with mine, making her taste her cum on me. When my movements became sporadic, she took over, holding me still, my hips hovering above her, and fucking me with her fingers, her thumb circling my clit in tight circles.

When I came, she kept going with her hand. The room filled with the wet sound of her fingers in my pussy. Tilting my head back, I squeezed my eyes shut, clenching around her fingers and twitching and jolting with every flick of her thumb over my clit that drew out my orgasm.

She kept going, and I'm sure she was trying to torture me with pleasure the way I had her. But I wasn't human, it didn't work on me. I could ride out that orgasm until her hand cramped and keep going. I kept my eyes shut, knowing the yellow had taken over as I lost control, crying out as I came again around her fingers.

Ilsa withdrew her hand, dipping her fingers into her mouth before pushing them into mine. I sucked on her fingers gratefully, groaning against her skin as she fucked them into my mouth, holding my chin with her other hand. She stared at me, her eyes widening at the way I worked my tongue around her wet fingers. When she pulled her hand from my mouth, I gasped and pressed a finger to her lips as she went to speak, shushing her gently.

Leaning forward, I placed a trail of kisses along her neck and jawline, guiding her to lie down before I dropped down next to her and pulled her against me.

She was so hot, her skin burning even as she fell asleep, reminding me of home.

CHAPTER 12

ILSA

The bed was cold. I had fallen asleep warm and comfortable, and now the space next to me had a chill to it as though no one had been there all night.

Was it a dream? Being with Ray?

Rolling over, I stared at the empty expanse of the bed next to me. I had given in to the temptation of her last night, and I'm not sure what I expected to happen today. But at the very least, I thought I'd wake up to find her next to me, still naked, perhaps ready to go again. The bed was empty, and it bothered me when it should've been something I rejoiced in. Although our coupling was brief, I had forgotten my injury at that time, not even giving it a second thought. Ray had made me feel desired and fueled my need for more.

And she wasn't even human.

But now she was gone from my bed, and I didn't know what to think.

Chances are, she was in the apartment somewhere. It didn't make sense for her to leave, but still, the symbolism of her not being next to me spoke worlds.

Honestly, what the hell did I expect? It was just another part of her game, life being one big playground to her.

Because she's a fucking demon, I needed to keep reminding myself of that.

It doesn't matter that she looks and talks and feels like a human because, underneath her skin, she isn't. We fucked, and that's all there was to it, nothing beyond physical pleasure and release, and once we figured out who Ray had pissed off, then she could go on her way, and I'd never have to see her again.

Why was it bothering me?

I couldn't shake the sense she wasn't a bad person, and while her views and motivations were skewed, she wasn't intentionally going around harming innocent people. It was a whole world of gray, and in a place where simple black and white barely exists anymore, I shouldn't be surprised.

But there were complications, and there was... *this.*

Whatever this was.

Rolling out of bed, I snatched a spare towel from

the walk-in closet and wrapped it around my body. I don't know where my tank top had gone, and I certainly wasn't going to stroll out there naked.

She might attack me.

Fuck or fight.

My skin tingled at the thought of tempting the demon out to play again.

Fuck.

"Morning!" Ray called cheerily from the kitchen as I nipped past.

"Morning," I muttered, ducking into the bathroom and closing the door behind me, the lock sliding into place with a click.

Why was I embarrassed and acting like a teenager who had been caught making out in the back seat of a car?

Dropping the towel to the floor, I studied my wounds in the mirror. They weren't great, but they would heal, and I could deal with the discomfort in the meantime. Stepping into the hot shower, I could only hope the water would wash away the feeling of her hands on my body.

But that was simply another lie I told myself.

When I stepped into the living room, rubbing my hair dry with a towel, I immediately realized where my tank top had gone because Ray was wearing it. However, she was bustier than I, and the fabric stretched over her chest, the straps straining against her shoulders. I wished I didn't notice, but it was hard not to.

I wished I didn't want to take it off her and not so I could have it back.

"Sleep well?" She grinned, cradling a mug between her hands containing what I deduced was coffee from the strong aroma.

"You going to give me a cup of my own coffee?" I asked, pointing.

She held out a mug, waiting until I came to her, and pulled it back at the last second so my hands grasped at the empty space where it had been. Playing children's games, I see. With her free hand, Ray tapped her cheek, turning her head and pouting. When I didn't move, her eyes shifted to the side, watching me.

"I can wait all day, sweets, and you know I'm strong enough to withhold this coffee from you."

She was grating against me again, and I ground my teeth together before planting a quick kiss on her cheek. Her smile was wide with superiority as she handed me the mug, and I almost gagged on the bitterness of the coffee as it simultaneously burned my tongue.

"A kiss for *this?* Doesn't seem like I got a good trade."

She licked her lips, her eyes flashing. "Do you want me to kiss you somewhere else to make up for it?"

I felt a rush of warmth between my legs at the memory of the extended orgasm she had pulled from me, almost painful in the pleasure. Ray had kept going until almost every drop of energy had been drained from my body. It felt like minutes, but even if it was thirty seconds, it was still the longest and most intense fucking orgasm I've ever had in my life, and I was getting wet simply thinking about obtaining that level of pleasure again.

Ray bit her lip, her eyes dropping to my pants before back up to my face, and I knew she sensed what I was thinking.

"Some sugar in the coffee will do," I said dryly. Ray had already gotten the upper hand, planting her dominance with the kiss-for-a-coffee move, and I didn't like how this dynamic was developing. I needed to regain some ground here.

"You sing in the shower."

Her statement threw me, and I stared at her blankly for a moment before bringing myself back to reality. "Yeah, didn't know you could hear me."

She laughed. "It was cute. I haven't heard the song before."

""Daydream Believer." My mum used to sing it to me."

"Is she dead?" Ray bit her lip, adding quickly, "I'm sorry, I didn't mean for it to sound so harsh."

Pursing my lips, I waited a beat before I responded. This wasn't really a topic I wanted to get into at all, let alone with Ray. "No, both my parents are alive, I just don't see them anymore."

"Why?"

"What's with all the questions?"

Ray leaned on the counter, resting her chin in her hands. "I'm curious about you."

Sighing, I mirrored her posture.

Fine.

"My dad was military as well. When I was medically discharged, I might as well have been a deserter in his eyes. Either you die on the field or you retire with style, and anything else is a disappointment." Why was I telling her this? I hadn't spoken to anyone about this other than Kelly, and even then, I hadn't given her much more than enough well-chosen words to get her to leave the topic alone. "My mom's Columbian. Dad was never happy his genes didn't steamroll over hers with me like they did with my brothers. I look like Mom, my brothers all look like Dad. I was doomed to be a disappointment from the start."

"I like your sexy caramel skin," Ray purred.

I snorted. "Can you not compare my skin to food,

please, demon?”

Ray purred again, making some throwaway comment about *eating me up* which I chose to ignore. Ray continued, “So, your dad was a high rank then.” She tapped her chin, and I wondered what she was thinking.

“You don’t get much higher.”

“Why doesn’t your mom leave him if he treats her like he does you?”

I eyed her. “No one says no to the General.”

“You did.”

I didn’t need to say *and look where it got me.*

Living on the wrong end of the city, spending my nights tracking down demons.

We stared at each other for a beat. Ray shuffled around a bit, seemingly unsure as to what to say. There was nothing she could say anyway. I shrugged and straightened, reaching for the cupboard to fetch the sugar. She had asked, and I had answered. I didn’t need her sympathy.

“Ray, we need to figure out who you’ve pissed off,” I said.

“Who I pissed off… *this year*?”

My lip twitched. “Yeah, let’s start with that.”

“So, what’s the plan?” Ray asked, sliding up next to me as I stirred sugar into the bitter mess she called coffee, her shoulder bumping mine. She was so relaxed as though nothing had transpired between us. Perhaps to her, it was nothing more than pleasure, so I supposed it made sense I looked at it the same way.

Normally, not a problem for me. But Ray was a puzzle I was apparently determined to solve.

"We search for links between the places you've targeted, find out who runs them."

She made a face. "I don't think I can remember them all."

"It's fine. I have notes."

"Oh yes, you've been stalking me. I forgot."

I raised my eyebrows at her. "I prefer investigating, but yes, I guess so." She smirked again, and while I fought to keep a neutral expression, I knew a twitch of my lip betrayed me. "You deserved it, though."

"Never said I didn't." She grinned.

Christ, she was intoxicating but also cheeky and a troublemaker. I'd have my hands full as long as she was staying with me.

Speaking of hands being full...

My eyes shifted to her chest again, and I shook the thought from my mind. Not soon enough, though, judging by the look on her face. Once again, she knew exactly what I had been thinking.

Tipping the coffee into the sink, the sugar unable to save it, I dropped the mug in after it before heading to the coffee table, tossing papers to the side until I found the map I had made tracking Ray's whereabouts.

"Wow, you *have* been busy," Ray said as I sat at the breakfast bar before unrolling the map. Ray shook her empty mug after staring at my handiwork. "Mind if I have some more coffee?"

"Go for it," I muttered, not looking up again.

Searching for patterns on the map, I put it together with what I had learned doing online research and asking around the streets while I tried to track Ray down in those first weeks. It was difficult to track who owned the businesses Ray had targeted, and to her credit, it did seem that it was almost completely random—no wonder the authorities thought it was a gang-war issue. The ownership of the buildings was tangled in layers upon layers of business names to protect the not-so-innocent, and I had learned more by asking people who were willing to talk on the street than I had from the internet.

Attempting to color code with only three different pens, I got to work. Looking up when there was an odd noise from the kitchen, I found Ray with a spoon in her mouth. She paused, sucking on the spoon, eyes widened slightly from the look I gave her like she had been busted doing something she shouldn't.

"Are you..." my gaze flitted from the jar in her hand to the spoon in her mouth, "... eating dry instant coffee?"

"Yeah," she mumbled, the word muffled around

the spoon before she withdrew it from her mouth with a pop. "Is that a problem?"

"Ah, I guess not?"

I pulled a face as she took another spoonful, shoving it in her mouth before coming and sitting next to me.

"Whoa, look at all the places I hit," she exclaimed, pride emanating through her voice. "Go me."

"This isn't something to be proud of."

"Isn't it?" She swept the empty spoon across the map. "Look at all these criminal bases that are now out of commission thanks to me."

It was hard to argue with that, so I didn't.

"It's not your place to make those decisions."

She scoffed. "We've had this discussion. Your justice system is corrupt, and half your police force is probably in the pockets of the criminals. I'm cutting out the middleman and having some fun in the process."

"You can't go around doing whatever you want. There are consequences."

"Like what? I wanted you, and I did you."

Flushing, I looked back at the map. "Consequences like getting shot or getting someone innocent attacked in an alleyway." I felt her body language change as her shoulders dropped.

"You're right, I didn't want that to happen."

"Which part?"

She had started sucking on the spoon again even

though it was empty. "All of it." We watched each other for a beat before she pointed to a building circled in red. "What's this?"

"A nightclub, Urban."

"Oh yeah, I know that place. There are a lot of shifty fucks around there. It was on my hit list, but there's always so much security. It would take a lot to get through, even for me."

"I think it's the base for some crime lord or something from what I've been told, cost me a fuckload of cash bribes to get that information, people were *not* willing to talk about it. I'm guessing they might own a lot of the places you targeted, intentional or otherwise." I looked up from the map, rubbing my eyes when the colors started to blur together. "I mean, you probably pissed off every crime syndicate in the city, but this one sounds like the biggest."

"Crime lord, eh? Like a real-life movie," Ray cried.

She sounded so excited I felt the corner of my lips lift into a grin. "I don't know what else to call it, okay? What's the correct terminology for this?"

Ray shrugged. "Let's just go with crime lord. It sounds cool."

"All right, wouldn't be worth doing this if it didn't sound cool."

"You get it." She winked at me and ignored my sarcasm as I shook my head. "So we just... head down there?"

It was my turn to shrug. "Sure, why not? Got to start somewhere, but I doubt they'll be open until later, though."

"I dunno. If there's someone in there worth seeing, they might be there outside of opening hours. Doing *business.*"

"That's almost a useful insight."

She poked my eyebrows where they furrowed with the spoon, giggling that laugh of hers, the one I still felt didn't match her look or demeanor. But now, it was hard to imagine her laughing any other way. "Don't sound so surprised." Ray winked again. "But..." she added, popping the spoon back in her mouth, "... if you're worried there'll be no one worth seeing there, I'm sure we can find some way to keep ourselves occupied for a few hours."

As she spoke, Ray stepped closer to me, and I froze, my stomach a mixture of fear and arousal. I couldn't deny we had chemistry, chemistry which exploded in mind-blowing sensations last night, but it must have been due to her nature. There simply can't be any other explanation. Because now, in the light of day, I couldn't get the word out of my head.

Demon.

Ray wasn't human but a supernatural being. The things of nightmares, and—I swallowed heavily, remembering the sensations of her mouth— apparently also of dreams. What happened last night can't happen again, and I can't allow myself to become clouded to what she really is.

Demon.

Her body language changed as she reacted to mine. I couldn't control the tensing of my shoulders and back, and there was a pang of guilt in my chest at the way her face dropped. Ray didn't back away from me. If anything, she seemed to edge closer and leaned forward slightly so she crowded into my space. A frown began to cloud her otherwise curious expression as she studied me, and I rubbed my arms before crossing them over my chest. She had a knack for making me feel small and weak—taking control in the bedroom I could handle, but the way she intimidated me now with her sheer presence, I hated it. I spent years building myself up to be as strong as my brothers, stronger even, and although none of it meant anything to them before or after my discharge, I wasn't afraid of anybody.

Until now.

Until Ray.

Worse was I *wasn't* scared of her, not really. But I was of what she represented, of a world that most humans live in blissful ignorance of, and I wished I could go back to being oblivious.

Demon.

The reminder was strong in my mind, and I couldn't shake it. I didn't *want* to shake it. I *needed* the constant replay of the truth in my head and the surge of fear when she stepped too close.

The adrenaline rush that spiked when her skin brushed mine I put down to being in a defensive mode, something I switched to on instinct now after years of training.

Although the warmth between my thighs screamed otherwise.

Ray was a demon from Hell.

And I couldn't let her be any more than that.

CHAPTER
13

RAY

Hot and cold is what I was getting from Ilsa. A fat lot of fucking nothing.

Hell, I didn't expect her to be fawning over me following our romp, but I thought at least it might have loosened her up a bit, endeared me to her, and let her know that she could trust me. Maybe pushed her to look past the whole *demon* thing. There were moments where her true self peeked through, a dry sense of humor and wit that she let slip before she brought herself back into line again.

Oops, can't reveal too much to the demon!

As if I hadn't already been in her bed.

It was me. She was still afraid of me, and I must admit, it pissed me off somewhat.

If I wanted to kill her, I'd had many chances to do so before now. So what was she so fucking upset about? Because I was a *demon?* Get over it. I was goddamn adorable.

It clawed at me something fierce that Ilsa was putting up such walls between us. I'm surprised my eye wasn't twitching from irritation every time I saw her spine straighten. I don't know how she expected us to work together to sort this out if she wouldn't talk to me properly and at least try to relax around me.

She'd relaxed last night, that was for goddamn sure. The way her body had gone limp after I teased the orgasm from her, drawing it out until she was a panting mess, was ecstasy in itself. I could've done anything with her in those vulnerable moments where she was a limp ragdoll of pleasure.

All I wanted to do was take her there again.

Ilsa didn't have to love me, but I wouldn't settle for this icy shit either.

Perhaps she hadn't figured out how persistent I could be yet.

We walked down an almost deserted street, the sunlight reflecting off every other shop window making me wish I'd snatched a pair of sunglasses from somewhere. On this end of the city, at this time of day, there wasn't much reason for people to be out and about. Those who had jobs to attend would already be there, and those who didn't would be sleeping off their ministrations from the previous night.

This entire end of the city smelled like sex, alcohol, danger, and fear, and I loved it.

"So this club—"

"Urban," Ilsa added.

"Urban, right." Like it mattered at all what it was called. "What uh… exactly is our plan again?"

"I thought you wanted to wing it?"

There was that curve of her lips again before she'd blink and shake her head slightly, then returned to her deadpan expression. I didn't like that expression on her—it looked too forced. Despite years of practice, she still hadn't mastered it naturally, remaining neutral. She was too expressive, a smile belonged on her face, or at least the curve of her lips that hinted at the cheeky nature I knew lay beneath the tough exterior. She'd let it slip around me already with her smart-ass quips and comments. I knew her better than she thought I did.

Keeping a mask on at all times required a lot of work, and it got old pretty fast.

I'd know.

Giggling, I answered, "Yeah, and it sounds like we're full-blown winging it. We're literally going to just stroll right up to the club? Doesn't seem like you at all."

"I'm simply going to ask to speak to whoever is in charge."

"And if that doesn't work?"

"I'm going to tell them who you are."

I stopped walking for a beat before rushing to catch up with Ilsa as she continued her long strides, every other stride hitching as her leg got the better of her. Her lip would twitch in irritation, but she wouldn't slow down, making no leeway for herself.

She walked with such purpose with those camo pants and heavy boots. It was sexy as fuck.

"You're going to turn me in?" I asked, coming up next to her.

As she stopped, I had to come back a few steps after realizing she was no longer walking next to me.

"They know who you are, Ray. They're going to recognize you anyway," she said, a hand on her hip.

Then her expression fell.

The words hit her at the same time they did me—it was written all over her face.

"So..." I said, licking my lips, "... we could be walking straight into a death trap? The club could be less of a source of information and more the exact place we shouldn't be going."

Ilsa stared at me. I could almost see her mind working. Like this was something which hadn't occurred to her, and honestly, up until this moment, it hadn't crossed my mind either. I was so invested in *her* that I hadn't thought much about the situation itself. Ilsa was looking at me with something that resembled accusation, as though she blamed me for her not thinking straight. Planning was her thing, not mine. I followed her, assuming she knew what she was doing.

Maybe I scrambled her brain with that orgasm last night.

"Shit," Ilsa muttered before leaning against the wall of a nearby building and shoving her hands in her pockets, falling into thought. I wanted to say something, anything to contribute, but all that crossed my mind were images of breaking the front door down and roundhouse kicking me some bad guys. So I said nothing. Occasionally, Ilsa would cast me another look, suggesting this was my fault, then press her lips together as her train of thought moved on.

As though I was to blame for her lapse in judgment.

Maybe I was.

After a while, Ilsa's eyes raked my body, and I'm not sure the look was entirely innocent. There was a pause, and then she was staring straight at me again, but her eyes had shifted out of focus. I took this to mean she was formulating a plan and decided to let her do whatever.

The silence was killing me. I wished she'd say something.

I only wanted this over with because being shot at with silver bullets had disrupted my fun.

Although being with Ilsa had opened up a new

world of entertainment, and maybe I didn't want that part to be over just yet.

"Can you change your appearance?" she asked me abruptly.

"Na, my human form is what it is. I can't change it. I can turn into a bat, though."

"Really?

I snorted. "No."

She didn't laugh.

Ilsa started gnawing on her bottom lip, and I tried to maintain my concentration on the situation at hand rather than her lips. Being with Ilsa the night before had served only to stir up my demon rather than satiate it, and with every passing moment—especially in the silence where I was left alone with my thoughts—it was clawing harder against me, straining to get out and take her again. Controlling my demon had been more difficult to maintain as the days stretched on than I had anticipated. Demons lived here for decades, so how did they do it? I'd need an outlet soon. Something, anything to take my mind off the woman in front of me. Because as it were, I'd either need to take her right here in the street or unleash some sort of bloodlust.

I know which I preferred, but I didn't think Ilsa would appreciate the public display.

"Surveillance."

"Sorry?" I was snapped out of my thoughts, and

she arched a brow at me.

"Surveillance. We watch them, see who's coming and going."

"And then what?" I asked.

"How about just one step at a time? We need to gather more information. These people don't exactly make themselves easy to find."

Impatience was edging in on her tone, and I grinned. It was so tempting to push her. She was so cute when she was mad—except for those times when she was flailing a silver knife about, that was less cute. But I guess I should keep the peace with Ilsa, at least for now. She was trying to help me, after all. Even though in the process, she was helping herself. I wanted to believe that somewhere underneath the bravado, she cared for my well-being.

After a beat, Ilsa nodded, more to herself than to me, and began striding toward the club again. I followed, catching up with her and occasionally casting her an unrequited glance, hoping she'd let me in on whatever secret plan she had beyond watching the club. But she said nothing.

When we reached Urban, Ilsa kept walking, circling the block twice from different angles—once passing the front of the club and another slipping down a side thoroughfare before coming around on the other side of the street. We were concealed mostly from the view of the club by the shop front verandas, sticking to the shadows. Following her lead, we finally slid down into a crouch, concealed by empty tables bolted to the concrete outside a café that was long shut down.

Falling into silence, we stared up at the second and third stories of our target building. Large windows adorned the side of the second story, but the third was closed off with shutters. I knew this club. I'd been in it once or twice the first few times I had come to Earth, drawn to it by the crowd that frequented—those who were worth robbing, getting their kicks by leaving the other end of the city and partying on the *wild side,* and those who robbed.

It was the type of place people came to be seen with its heavy, smoky atmosphere, loud music, expensive drinks, and seductive décor. Or sometimes, not to be seen but to be lost in the crowds while they had business to do. There was a balcony that overlooked the dance floor and some sort of VIP area up there I could never gain access to no matter how much I batted my eyelashes and pushed my tits together at the bouncer.

Ilsa slid down next to me, her forearms resting on her knees, staring at the building, almost appearing to take inventory of it.

She impressed me. I was happy to let Ilsa take control of the situation. For now, anyway. If we got into trouble, I was certain I could fight my way out, and she knew how to handle herself well enough. While I tended to rely on humans underestimating me and not suspecting I was as strong as I was, Ilsa was different. She may not have been a physically imposing woman, but she looked the part—toned body, a stern expression, and radiating power.

Sexy as fuck.

It didn't escape me how she tried to hide her limp as she walked and took long, purposeful strides. An impressive specimen of a woman, she'd captured my attention in such a way I found myself hoping this investigation stretched out, wishing we wouldn't find whoever was trying to harm us straight away, and maybe, with time, she'd relax around me. Because her shoulders were tense, and she always looked as though she was on the verge of leaping into a defensive pose at any moment, pulling another silver knife from some hidden pocket.

It may have been an immature wish, but I didn't care.

I liked her like a cat was attracted to the one person in the room who doesn't like cats.

My attraction to her, coupled with her strength and attitude, was magnified by the animalistic lust that had exploded from both of us in bed together.

At the memory, my demon stirred, and I had to suppress the growl threatening to burn in my throat. My skin started to ripple, my shoulders flexed, and my neck cracked as I shifted. Learning my mistakes too late, as usual, it was a slap in the face now that I couldn't control my demon through violence alone—we needed both, *craved* both the fight and the fuck. Demons were instinctual beings, and if our minds denied us what we desired, they would take over and claim it.

Shit.

It was coming.

CHAPTER 14

ILSA

Ray had been glancing at me as we worked our way around to a place from which we could observe the club, and I know she was dying to know what my plan was.

There was no way to tell her I didn't have one.

Because I was well out of my depth.

I was a soldier. I went where I was told, did the job, and left. I could make tactical decisions on the ground—gather intel, know the terrain and territory, then make a decision. Planning ahead too far didn't work because you could never really know what the next few minutes held. Ray looked at me as though I were a detective or a cop like she had lumped all authority figures together in the same basket, assuming we all had the same skill set.

I'm not stupid. I could've progressed through the

ranks, but I didn't want to. This was something else my father had seen as a weakness, but I saw only as control over my own life. I didn't want to be the one sitting in an office giving commands. I needed to be there, on the field, to see the innocent people and have the constant reminder shoved in my face of why I was doing what I did. Because if I didn't have that, if the people were reduced to nothing but words and numbers on a screen, and if I could tell someone to pull a trigger rather than doing it myself, then I might lose my humanity.

Like he had.

So, I had no real plan. This was my terrain now, though. I had cased the building and knew enough about what went on inside to know these people were either a threat or a very useful source of information. I had also put faith in the fact that between Ray and me, if shit went down, we were strong enough to get ourselves out of the situation.

Observation was necessary. It may not be the mile-a-minute thrill ride Ray was hoping, judging by her constant fidgeting and twitching, but it was needed.

It grated against me that I hadn't considered the person trying to kill us could be in the club when we had started walking there. They could've recognized us as soon as we walked through the damn door. Whoever they were, they, of course, knew what Ray looked like, even if they didn't know her name because simply seeing us together was enough for them to turn on me.

What seemed so fucking obvious now slid past my thought process *because* of her. She had infiltrated my mind, and I could barely concentrate just looking into those golden eyes of hers, let alone when her body heat was pressed against mine.

We were here too early. I knew there wouldn't be anything going on at this time of day, but I couldn't stay in the apartment with Ray—she was too much of a temptation.

Christ, and here I thought the girls I went for before were bad girls.

A fucking demon.

Shaking my head, I still couldn't get my mind fully around it. Every nerve in my body was on edge, and every now and then she'd cast me a glance, her eyes wide and hopeful. Ray had a strange innocence about her, discovering a world and still learning the consequences. I didn't know what she wanted from me. Reassurance? A more stable plan? A teenage make-out session?

To fuck in the street?

Barely catching the shudder before it ran down my spine, I managed to stay still. Much too much of a temptation. How could a demon be cheeky and sweet and funny and still be... a *demon?*

Glancing at her at the same time she looked at me, we locked eyes for a moment. I couldn't pull my gaze from hers, and she certainly wasn't going to be the first to look away. There was a world of questions swimming in my mind which I could be using this time to ask her. Questions about the universe and life which she'd know the answers to. Questions about places that I hoped I'd never see, about Heaven and Hell and the way everything worked and fit together. In this world where humanity was ignorant of everything that existed outside our immediate lives, she held the truth that none of us ever thought we'd get close to until it was too late to tell anyone.

But I couldn't.

Because asking her, hearing her talk about those things, would make this all the more real, and as weak as it made me feel, I genuinely didn't think I could take it. Maybe it wasn't weakness. Maybe it was simply humanity. Were we meant to know the answers to the *big questions*?

Ray and I had become tangled up together when all I had wanted to do was save people from getting hurt or killed through collateral damage to whatever mission she was on. But now, her safety and mine were on the same line, and we had to figure this out together—demon or not.

She was still staring at me.

Beyond all that—as if it could get any worse— was my undeniable attraction to her. An animalistic lust I've never experienced before. Ray assured me those feelings were driven purely by my desire for her, originating from inside me and not because she was using some demon tricks to make me feel this way. Could she do that? Make the warmth spread between my legs and have my clit throb with need whenever she looked at me? But I had to tell myself Ray must be lying because that's what demons do, right? Because I couldn't accept these feelings were anything other than the weakness of the flesh giving in to a power and instinct I'd never understand.

But still, I kept remembering the feel of her on me, of my fingers inside her, and her coming around me.

Intoxicating.

Biting my bottom lip, I was about to tear my eyes from hers when she growled.

Low and menacing, building from the back of her throat and rumbling through those perfect lips. The growl kept going, and she bared her teeth as a flash of yellow passed across her eyes.

My eyes widened, and Ray looked hastily at the ground, but her shoulders were trembling.

Was she crying?

"What's the matter?" I asked. "Do you have a stomachache from eating instant coffee grounds?"

"Quiet."

I leaned away from her at the command. The voice wasn't her own. It was scratchy and grating like it was spoken in two octaves at the same time. It was partially the voice I knew—her human voice—and something else.

Something I didn't want to know about.

"Ray—" My words were cut off with a gasp when she raised her head. Her eyes were a blazing yellow with those black slits for pupils darting madly around before settling on me.

"Stop saying my name!" she screeched, and I scrambled to move away from her. Her skin was changing as though her veins were once again filled with the black ink I had witnessed the first time I saw her. Every vein darkened and widened before the inky color would spill out. Uneven patches of black formed and spread, sending it around underneath her skin in cobwebs that tangled together when they reached each other.

What would happen when the black took over all her skin?

Then there were small lines of glowing red, weaving their way between the black.

Staying in a defensive crouch, I shifted along the wall away from her, digging in my pocket and drawing out a silver knife. I knew now it wouldn't kill her, and somehow that made it easier to draw on her. Because even as the fear pulsed through me as I watched her muscles ripple underneath her skin, I didn't want to kill her. Because somewhere in there was Ray.

There was pain and fear in her eyes, and all I wanted to do was help.

With an unnaturally fast movement of her neck, Ray turned to me, her eyes flashing dangerously. She didn't even acknowledge the knife, her eyes burning into only mine, and like a wave, it crashed over me—my impulsive reaction to her instinct. My attraction to the Ray I was getting to know overwhelmed me when it was coupled with whatever demon shit was going on with her now. Something dark and dangerous sparked through the air between us.

When fear should've been the dominant reaction, underneath the fear was arousal.

With a growl, she was on me, and when her body slammed into mine and I hit the ground, I dropped the knife, hearing it clatter across the pavement as her hands grabbed my wrists. Her lips found mine, and I tried to protest before her tongue was in my mouth, and her hips ground obscenely against me.

Crying out when she sunk her teeth in my neck, I struggled against her grip on my wrists and said her name over and over again, trying to snap her out of this, whatever this was. Because while my fear mingled with my arousal, creating a confusing and heated sensation across my body, I was aware of what she was capable of doing.

How much control did she have like this? Not much judging by the snarling and rough handling, and I couldn't be sure she wouldn't kill me, accidentally or otherwise.

Would I have the strength to save myself if she tried to kill me in a frenzy?

"Every time you say my name..." she snarled then continued, "... it drives me wild." The otherworldly tone to her voice still present, I trembled under her touch, and she nipped and bit her way along my shoulder and collarbone. "I can feel your need. I need this too."

For a moment, our eyes locked, and a glimpse of the white of her human eyes peeked through. "I'm sorry," she whispered, and the pain in her voice broke me before it was gone, replaced with another growl. Ray shifted so both my wrists were trapped in the vice-like grip of one of her hands, and her fingers trailed down my body, fighting with the button and zipper on my pants before she pushed her palm between my legs. When she dipped a finger inside me, she bared her teeth, and I whimpered as she roughly pumped her finger in and out. She had made me wet, and I could feel the warmth flush around her hand. When Ray opened her eyes, they were still yellow, and her teeth found my neck again, biting hard enough to draw blood.

Gritting my teeth through the pain, I began struggling anew against her grip. Ray was licking my neck, inching closer to the wound she had just made. Somehow, I knew what she was going to do, and I didn't want it. Not some vampire shit.

"Please," I said, renewing my struggles against her. "Don't kill me."

Ray froze, slowly lifting herself until she was looking into my eyes. I blinked hard, hoping she didn't see the beginnings of tears forming. With a shake of her head, her eyes switched between human and demon before they returned to their normal color. She was snarling again, jolting and convulsing on top of me, and slowly the black ink began fading from her skin.

Ray recoiled from me, scrambling along on the pavement before pushing herself against the wall and hugging her arms around her knees. I remained still, slowly lowering my aching arms and doing up my pants. My clit was pulsing from the loss of sensation of her palm, and I hated that I wanted more.

"I wasn't going to kill you," Ray muttered against her legs.

The conflicting emotions stirred within me. She looked so broken. But a moment before, she had been a raging beast, playing my body like an instrument and responding with her own instinct. The combination of fear and arousal left me feeling empty and weak, and I was torn between wanting to comfort her and yell at her.

Retrieving the knife, I shoved it back in my pocket, and she followed my motions. Keeping my distance from her, I crouched again, watching her cautiously, waiting for signs of another outburst and prepared to strike if I had to.

Would I follow through, though? Did I really want to attack her?

What scared me the most was I wanted to give myself to her. Deep inside, I wanted her to take me. I was responding to her on a level I didn't even know existed, and knowing I could draw that side out of her filled me with a sense of power and lust.

A part of her she obviously worked so hard to control came undone when she was around me.

And I liked it.

Cursing under my breath, I relaxed my pose and leaned against the wall, still keeping a few feet between us.

Just in case.

CHAPTER
15

ILSA

"What the fuck was that, Ray?" I asked after a few minutes of silence, trying to keep my voice as calm as possible.

"I'm sorry." Her voice sounded weak, quiet, not like her at all. "I lost control."

"No shit." Rage bubbled in my stomach, but I managed to keep it controlled—a lifetime of experience. "Why did it happen? And how do I know it won't happen again? Have I got to be on constant alert around you? Because we're supposed to be working together to keep safe."

Ray eyed me out of the corner of her eye, keeping her lips pressed against her knees with her legs drawn up to her chest, her toes bouncing as she rested her pinpoint heels on the concrete. "It's your fault."

Tilting my chin to my chest, I looked at her in disbelief as my eyebrows raised, unsure if I had heard her correctly. "I'm sorry, what?"

Ray shifted until she was cross-legged. "It's you. I lost control because of you. I could feel your arousal, you were thinking about fucking me, and it was practically *oozing* from you." I stared at her but couldn't find anything to say. She shrugged a shoulder. "I've tasted you, and I want more. I have instincts I have to unleash, or they'll take me over."

Touching my neck, my fingers came away dotted with blood. In the space of a moment, her eyes flashed yellow before she blinked it away. When I recoiled from her, she dropped her gaze to the ground.

"I was never going to kill you." She sighed before glaring at me. "I see you still carry a silver knife, though. Where's the trust, huh?"

"It's a necessary precaution, apparently."

"But you didn't know that when we left your place. I thought we'd made progress."

I scoffed quietly, progress toward what? What exactly did she think was happening here? But I didn't want to ask in case her answer reflected the thoughts I didn't want to acknowledge.

"I'm sorry I didn't tell you about the knife."

She stared at me. "I'm sorry I scared you."

"Don't you mean you're sorry for attacking me?"

Grinning, Ray intentionally stared back at the nightclub. I had almost forgotten about it and why we were here.

Oh my God, I hope no one saw us grinding against each other on the pathway.

Fuck.

"No," she said. "I'm not sorry for that part." The look she gave me... fuck, if I weren't sitting down, I'm sure my legs would've buckled. "Because you were so wet. You can't hide your desires from me."

I wanted to argue but couldn't find it in myself to do so. Instead, I simply stared at the club with her, keeping my hand on the knife in my pocket.

Just in case.

Although I knew if she lost control again, I wouldn't use it.

I wasn't a submissive person, but she made me want to submit to her.

Nothing happened, and it started to grow warm even in the shade of the shops. A handful of people came and went, and no one gave us a second glance. I had kept a few feet between Ray and me, but at least on the outside, it seemed she had herself under control now and was apparently completely apathetic at having lost control in the first place.

When the club's door opened, I sat up straight, scrambling to my feet when I realized the man who had exited the club was coming our way. He was huge, tattoos snaking across his arms and disappearing under his fitted t-shirt before continuing up his neck. It was a colorful assortment of random images which I assumed meant nothing, but perhaps I was being judgmental. His stride was casual, but it was hard not to feel as though I should be arming myself, and my fingers gripped the knife in my pocket.

Ray was on her feet, sliding over until she was by my side but half a step in front of me. I wasn't even sure if she was aware she had done it. There was something touching about the small gesture.

Demon, Ilsa. Demon.

I kept reminding myself so as not to get in any deeper.

As if I weren't already past the point of no return.

The man from the club stopped on the street, keeping distance between us. "Boss wants to see you," he grunted.

"Why?" Ray barked out.

His lips lifted into a snarl. I guess that was his version of a smile. It was unsettling. "Two strangers sitting here for hours watching the place after practically fucking each other in broad daylight raises some concerns..." he smirked again, "... and curiosities."

"What if we don't want to see the boss?" Ray jeered.

I tried to keep my expression neutral as Ray threw questions back at the man. He chuckled, crossing his arms over his impressive chest and raising a brow at us. "Ladies, you don't have a choice."

I almost suffocated, not releasing the sigh of relief I had been holding in my lungs when he had spoken.

Strangers.

Key word.

Guess they didn't know who we were after all. Hopefully, this wasn't all wasted time.

Ray turned and winked at me, and the bodyguard raised his brows. I widened my eyes in warning, pursing my lips, hoping she'd keep her mouth shut going forward. She acted as if this were some sort of game, but I guess I should be used to that by now with her. But we were searching for people who had made it quite clear they would kill us both if pushed further, so I'm not sure what part of that had escaped her attention.

He turned to face the street and stretched his arm out, indicating for us to walk. I didn't like the idea of him being behind us, but he was right—we didn't have a choice, not if we wanted to figure this thing out, and the thinly-veiled threat he had issued between the lines wasn't lost on me.

Although I suspected it was lost on Ray with how she bounced along in front of me as though we were about to take a tour of a chocolate factory.

At times like these, I tried to keep my limp to a minimum, not keen to show weakness. But it was difficult, especially following the stiffness in my legs from sitting on the pavement for so long.

When we reached the club, he moved swiftly in front of us, holding the door open and shooing us inside. The light from the sun was quenched immediately as he closed the heavy door with a thud, and the dim neon lighting added to the foreboding atmosphere of the place.

A nightclub in the daytime wasn't a sexy place.

What the fuck was I thinking coming here armed with only a tiny knife?

When I moved to ascend the stairs, he grabbed my shoulder. My immediate response was to whirl around and take on a defensive stance. He didn't flinch but did look mildly surprised.

"Hold your arms out."

"What?"

"I'm going to pat you down." His tone left no room for argument, and gritting my teeth against the world of responses filling my mind, I held my arms out and spread my legs slightly. He was all business, and I was thankful for that, at least. He didn't linger, not paying more than necessary attention to my chest, focusing more on my torso and thighs.

When he reached my pocket, I stiffened as he slid his hand inside, pausing and eyeing me before continuing and removing the silver knife. Surely, he wouldn't be offended by such a small weapon? But he studied it with interest, casting me a look I couldn't interpret before pocketing it himself.

I wanted to ask for it back since I was running out of the fucking things.

Ray couldn't wipe the grin from her face when he patted her down, and she moaned and writhed as he moved his hands over her body. I knew she was messing with him, but it still made me grind my teeth in irritation. When she looked at me with that smirk, I cringed, knowing exactly what she was doing, trying to get a rise out of me and to spark a hint of jealousy.

Dammit, it was working too.

"Upstairs, ladies," he said as though he were inviting us somewhere fun and exclusive and not to meet some underground crime lord.

Pressing my lips together in what I hoped passed for a smile, I moved up the stairs, Ray following close behind me.

CHAPTER 16

RAY

Ilsa hated this, hated every second we were in this club. I thought this is what she wanted, to investigate and follow through. Perhaps it was being disarmed by the bouncer, though I'm not sure what good that knife would've done her anyway. There were bound to be more guards upstairs.

When we reached the top of the stairwell, the door opened into a curved balcony overlooking the dance floor. Guess I finally got to see what was so special about the VIP area.

It was something special, all right.

Like recognizes like, and I knew another celestial being when I saw one.

No wonder the bouncer had taken such interest in Ilsa's choice of silver for a weapon.

Our crime boss sat in a velvety red chair, and

although there was another single chair and an empty couch, all the other men in the room stood around him. There was something off about the room's décor like it was chosen by someone trying too hard to show their financial status. It didn't match the man sitting in the chair, and my immediate instinct was he had taken ownership by force. Two bouncers flanked each side of him, another two stood in front of the door behind where he sat, and the one behind us closed the door to our exit with a click.

Seven, plus the man in the chair.

If we needed to, it might not be as easy to get out of here in a hurry as I had hoped.

I wondered if his men knew he wasn't human.

Should I tell Ilsa? She was already weary of me. Would that just set her off further?

Ilsa stood with her arms crossed over her chest. She still radiated authority, and it was exciting to witness. I considered mimicking her pose but realized if we came in here posing like some sort of boyband, it would only appear comical, and I doubted we looked threatening as it was. So I settled for dropping one hip and placing my hands on my waist. Ilsa's expression—a permanently arched brow—expressed *they* were somehow wasting *her* time. I was digging it.

"Who are you?" the man in the chair asked. There was no doubting the authority in his voice—deep and dark without having to raise the volume—it filled the space between us before filtering into our bodies. He wasn't shouting, he didn't need to. I bet you could hear that voice even when the club was in full swing, every word he said would pour right into your soul. I hated that I couldn't see his eyes. Who wore sunglasses inside anyway? What was he hiding?

Something I was sure of—there was power behind those glasses, centuries of power, and a darkness I wasn't sure even I'd mess with.

Although, that hadn't stopped me before.

"You first," Ilsa said. "You dragged us in here."

He chuckled. "*Dragged* seems like an exaggeration. I..." he circled his hand in the air, searching for the words, "... invited you without option."

"Diplomatic," Ilsa murmured, and credit to her, she didn't flinch when he slowly removed his sunglasses and danger flashed across his dark eyes. They were so dark, almost black, the pupil nearly indistinguishable from the iris. The sunglasses made sense—the reveal of those eyes would be a hell of an interrogation technique. He didn't look human even in his human form, his eyes offering a supernatural quality to his appearance. He'd be handsome if he didn't make my skin crawl.

He looked like fucking evil incarnate, and that was coming from *me*.

"Emrick," he said as he stood, placing a hand on his chest. "Please, sit down."

"I think we'd rather stand."

He studied Ilsa under his brow before closing the gap between them with a handful of casual strides. Nothing about Emrick said that he was in a hurry, but *everything* screamed that we were lucky simply to be alive in his presence.

Who the fuck was this guy?

He towered over Ilsa when they stood toe to toe, his chest heaving with every breath as though he was trying to control his patience.

Ilsa didn't know what he was or the fire she was playing with. How could she?

"Ilsa..." I started.

"Sit!" Emrick barked.

This time, Ilsa flinched before glaring at me as though her reaction was my fault. She eyed Emrick for a beat longer, staking her claim on the floor she stood on before slowly and without dropping his eye contact, moved and sat in the only single chair opposite his.

Emrick waited until I was seated on the couch before he returned to his spot, crossing one ankle over his knee and picking up a glass, swirling the contents while watching us.

When he smiled, it somehow made him look more dangerous.

"Why were you watching my club?" he asked,

still looking at the contents of his glass. I got the impression he didn't deem us worth his time.

I looked at Ilsa for guidance and found none as she was still staring hard at Emrick. "Information," she said. "Someone tried to kill us, and I thought you might know who."

"Why would I know that?"

"Because it has to do with the destruction of businesses that's been going on around here."

His eyes flashed with amusement, but when his gaze fell to me, I resisted the urge to shudder under his stare. He was all things darkness and power. A history of anger and pain lingered behind those eyes. Although he laughed as he indicated to me with his drink, splashing a portion of it onto the expensive carpet, I could feel it.

He *hated* me.

"Oh." He chuckled, waiting for the murmuring laughter from his comrades to die down. "You're the demon who's been burning down places." He eyed me again, and I frowned at him. "And very carefully not killing anyone," he muttered.

Ilsa said nothing, and I wondered if she put two and two together about his awareness of the rules I was bound by. I could hardly ask her. Slowly, he returned his gaze to Ilsa, holding it for a beat before looking back at me.

Apparently, once he realized who and what I was, he didn't deem talking to Ilsa worth his time.

Surely, he felt my presence when I entered?

Was I that weak to him?

"What's this human to you?" he asked. "A fuck toy?"

"Fuck you," Ilsa spat out, her cheeks flaming with rage as Emrick chuckled again. Placing his glass on a table, he snapped his fingers, and the bouncer closest to the door disappeared down the stairs, again locking the door behind him.

"I don't know for sure who tried to kill you, but I know who it was likely to have been."

"Who?" I asked.

"Not so fast..." he trailed off, staring at me while holding his palm out, waiting for me to speak.

"Ray," I offered.

"Ray," he repeated, the word as smooth as velvet and sweet as poison on his tongue. "What do I get in return for this information?"

"What do you want?" Ilsa asked.

He continued to look at me, directing his answer to me. This behavior wasn't out of respect but pure intimidation. "Nothing is for free in my business, ladies. Perhaps you can do me a favor."

It wasn't a question.

"What favor?" I questioned.

"No fucking way."

Glancing at Ilsa, we had spoken at the same time. I tried to communicate through a look what I wanted to say, but she only frowned at me.

"Ilsa, it's only fair," I murmured.

She scoffed. "You think men like this play fair?"

"You better watch your mouth," Emrick growled. "Or I'll fill it for you."

Ilsa stood, and with a firm hand on her shoulder, she was forced to sit. She slapped the bouncer's hand away, and he released her, but she didn't try to stand again.

"Favor for a favor." Emrick leaned back in his chair. "It's only fair," he added, grinning at Ilsa.

"What do you want?" she pushed out through gritted teeth.

"Oh, nothing right now." Ilsa's eyes flashed with rage at his answer, and this only served to increase the smirk on Emrick's face. "But when I need something, you'll be the first to know."

The bouncer who had gone down the stairs returned now, and Emrick fell silent as a waitress came into the room. She sashayed up to him and offered him a simpering smile which didn't travel to her eyes as she filled his glass.

Vodka.

Expensive.

Straight.

When she turned to leave, Emrick snatched at her wrist and forced her to bend so he could whisper in her ear. Her smile dropped, and her face lost its color, but she nodded before leaving faster than she had come in.

Emrick held his hand out, and the bouncer handed him a slip of paper, which he scribbled something on before sliding it across the table to me.

"This is the name and address of the man who owns a good number of those buildings. He would have been the one who tried to kill you." When I went to grab the paper, he gripped my wrist, and my eyes shot to his, almost getting lost in the darkness of his gaze and the aura of power radiating from him. It was beyond celestial power. It was a complete power over the men in this room, this building, and the city beyond. It was a reminder that fear of him was not only smart, it was necessary, and he was capable of terrible things.

Fear was a powerful tool.

I should know.

"You better be willing to put him out of the picture for good, Ray," he whispered. "You leave him alive, and he'll just keep coming after you." Leaning back, there was no smirk this time. "You should be more careful whose toes you step on in the city. You might upset the wrong people."

Nodding, I took the paper. When he had released my wrist from his grip, fear lurched in my stomach at the knowledge I wouldn't have been able to move if he hadn't have let me.

Ignoring Ilsa's protest, I grabbed her arm and dragged her out of the room and down the stairs without another word.

Emrick was powerful beyond anything I'd come across on Earth.

Powerful and dangerous.

And I'd hate to think what favor he'd seek from us when the time came.

CHAPTER 17

ILSA

Snatching the paper from Ray, I unfolded and studied it. This address wasn't marked on the map I had made, so whoever this was, he obviously kept himself below the radar.

"We need to be armed," Ray said, glancing back at the club.

"We can't kill him, Ray."

"No." She made a face, somewhere between a pout and a sneer. "I know, but we at least need to scare or fuck him up a bit. Then you can hand him over to your precious cops."

"Under what charge?"

"I have no idea. That's not my problem."

"It kind of *is* your problem."

"Whatever! We'll sort it out later." She scoffed as she was on edge. The exchange with Emrick had hardly been pleasant, but it seemed odd it had thrown her so much.

"Wing it again, you mean?" I asked.

"Sure, it's got us this far."

Stopping, I grabbed her arms and spun her to face me. "Is this really how you function? Just making shit up as you go along?"

She shrugged. "Well, yeah."

"Unbelievable."

"It's worked so far, hasn't it?"

Humorless laughter escaped me. "Oh, yeah! Really! Well... you've been shot, I've been jumped, and a man almost died. It's working a treat."

"*Almost* died, Ilsa. Key word."

Rolling my eyes, noticing she had glazed over the whole being shot thing, I turned and glanced down the street. She was right about one thing though, we'd need to be armed when we went to find this man. But we couldn't go in there guns blazing since that's how Ray had gotten into trouble in the first place.

"Well..." she started walking again, "... I'm going to go check it out. You can either come or not."

"Fine," I hissed through a murmur. "But don't blame me if everything turns to shit."

"I wouldn't dream of it." She giggled then, back to the Ray I knew.

"At least let me get some knives from home."

"I thought you didn't want to kill him?"

"I didn't say I was going to, I just don't want to go in there naked."

"Might distract him, though, if you were naked. I know it would distract me."

My mind flooded with the feeling of her on me, the flurry of her hands and teeth as she lost control.

"We don't need another incident like before," I said.

"I'll be good." She batted her eyelashes at me, and I huffed out an unamused breath through my nose.

"Yeah, right." I wasn't convinced.

Ray giggled again and led the way back to my apartment.

Flopping herself down onto the couch as if she owned the place, Ray stared at the ceiling and whined, "Do we need to go straight away?"

"Do you have somewhere else to be?" I asked, digging through my bags and grabbing a selection of knives I could conceal easily and one I didn't plan to.

I jumped when I felt her hands on my waist as I hadn't heard her approach. How the fuck did she move so quickly and silently in those heels?

"We've got unfinished business to take care of."

"I don't think we do," I said, brushing her hands away.

Remind yourself, woman.

Demon.

Unnatural.

Immoral.

Dangerous.

Demon.

On top of all the bad decisions I had made before, considering being with Ray was next-level shit.

She spun me around to face her, jolting her head out of the way as I turned, still clutching the knife I had picked up. The large butcher knife hovered between us, and Ray's eyes shifted from it to me and back again, but I couldn't put it down. The blade felt like a barrier between us, a wall that if I were to break it down, it would destroy whatever self-control I had left.

My resolve melted the moment she touched me.

She promised she wasn't using some demonic power shit on me.

She *promised* me.

Could I trust her, though?

Were these feelings really my own?

"I won't hurt you, Ilsa," Ray whispered. "I think you should know that by now."

"I do." I could barely breathe, and the lust that radiated from her body was so strong I could almost taste it.

"Put the knife down," she said.

When I didn't move, she ran her tongue up the blade, and my eyes widened. Ray wrapped her hands around mine, gently prying my fingers from the handle.

"Ray..." I was practically whimpering at this point. "What is this?"

She looked at me, and I know she knew what I meant.

What was happening between us?

What were these sensations?

Because although I thought I recognized them, it couldn't be possible, not with her, not these feelings.

Demon.

Love.

Please, don't let it be true.

"I don't know..." she confessed. "But of the two of us, you're the only one still fighting."

"How can I trust you?" I whispered.

Minutes ago, we were in a tense situation with a stranger, and now my body was filled with a different kind of intensity. Her lips, her eyes, her scent, everything about Ray was intoxicating—her smile, her laugh, hell, even her impulsiveness.

She removed the knife from my hands and placed it on the counter behind me. Her hips were against mine, pinning me in place.

"You still carry a silver knife, and I trust you."

"You do?" The words were almost nothing on the air between us.

"Of course." She smiled. "I can read you like a book."

This time when she kissed me, it was soft and gentle, a stark reflection from the urgency and violence of our last encounter, and I know she was trying to make up for it. Her lipstick smeared against my cheek as she dragged her lips across my face before kissing her way down my neck, gently kissing over the places she had bitten earlier.

"You don't have to be so gentle," I whispered, and she giggled again.

Facing me, she took my cheeks in her hands, forcing me to pout before pressing her lips to mine and grinning. "Oh, I'm not going to be. I know you like it rough, soldier, but I need you to know I *can* be gentle if you need me to be."

"I think I just need you."

"I *know* you need me." She kissed her way across my cheek again. "Who wouldn't?" Another kiss. "I'm fucking delightful."

Chuckling, I placed my hands on her hips and moved to push her away from me. I needed the space from her. I needed her not to be touching me because I couldn't concentrate when she did. The electricity between us was too much, and I felt more alive with her than I had in a long time. But she simply pressed against me harder, the counter pushing painfully into my lower back, the feel of her hips making me moan.

"Don't be under any illusions you're in control here, Ilsa," she muttered, biting at my earlobe and making me shudder. "You're mine."

Her kisses became urgent again, making my stomach flutter with the memory of her tongue between my legs, lapping at my sensitive clit and sending me over the edge.

"Do you have any toys?" she asked, and I nodded, making her giggle again. "Show me."

Testing the waters, I shifted again, and this time she let me move away from the counter before I had a chance to change my mind. I grabbed her hand and pulled her toward the bedroom. When I went to open a drawer, Ray shoved me out of the way, catching me with one arm when with her strength, she had made me lose balance on my leg.

"Sorry," she muttered.

My weakness was embarrassing, and it ignited a spark of resentment inside me, but I simply pushed my hair from my face and told her it was okay without making eye contact.

Ray stared at me, studying my expression until I looked into her eyes, checking for anger, I supposed. If there was any, it wasn't at her for playfully shoving me, it was at myself. Placing a hand on my chest, she pushed gently until I sat on the edge of the bed. Kneeling in front of me, Ray undid my boots and slid them off, followed by my socks and pants.

As she was sliding my boots off, she ran her hands over each of my feet in turn. "You think you deserve to wear these boots? You're just a human who likes to play with guns and knives." When the corner of my lip lifted in a scowl, the anger flaring in my eyes again, she smirked. Ray removed her shoes and pants, leaving her in a t-shirt and panties before pulling my boots over her feet and lacing them up. "I'm in charge today."

Ray stood and slammed the boot on the mattress between my spread legs. "Is that going to be a problem, soldier?" Her eyebrow arched, and when she first stood, I almost smiled with amusement. But for some reason, I shrunk under her gaze. Perhaps it was her using my humanity against me, her harsh comments coupled with the playful edge to her voice. I found myself staring at her legs, following the inviting line of her skin up to the lace of her underwear. When I reached out to touch her leg, she slapped my hand away before kneeling in front of me again.

"This drawer?" she asked, and I nodded. "Finish getting naked, soldier. I'm going to make a selection."

She was commanding, hints of a raw edge to her voice I'd heard only once before—when she had attacked me. Pulling my top over my head before unclasping and discarding my bra, I waited as she shuffled through my bottom drawer. The drawer I hadn't opened in much too long.

Without looking at me, she added, "Panties too. Don't make me punish you."

I felt the warmth flush between my legs.

Maybe I wanted her to punish me.

As though reading my mind, she glanced up at me, smirked as she took something out of the drawer and placed it by the side of the bed and out of my view.

Too entranced with watching her, I hadn't moved fast enough for her liking. With a snarl, Ray gripped at the sides of my underwear and yanked them down, forcing me to lie back on the bed before grabbing my hips and dragging me forward until my legs were dangling over the edge of the mattress, spread on either side of her shoulders.

On her knees, she brought her face between my legs again, her breath warm against my sensitive clit, causing me to shudder again.

"Keep those legs spread," she commanded, and I jumped when the cold touch of rubber slid between my waiting pussy lips. "How long has it been, soldier?" she asked, the devilish grin evident in her voice.

"Too long," I all but panted out.

"That's what I thought." And with that, she

pushed the dildo inside me, slowly but in one smooth motion, it filled me up. It wasn't large, but it didn't need to be. Curved at the end, it rubbed so perfectly against my G-spot I shuddered again when it was fully inside me.

"We're playing a different game today," she said as she began pumping it in and out of me. "You're going to come on demand, and if you don't, I'm going to tease you until you *beg me* for release."

Nodding, I spread my legs wider, crying out when she smacked my inner thigh.

"When I give you a command, you'll respond with *Yes, Drill Sergeant.*"

"Yes, Drill Sergeant." I moaned.

God, the army never felt so good. This was wrong on so many levels, and yet I was lapping up every bit of it, getting lost in the pleasure of her expert ministrations.

"Now listen closely. After my count, you're going to come on *one.*"

"Yes, Drill Sergeant," I gasped out as her lips found my clit once again, sucking at my bud and sending an explosion of pleasure through me.

"*Ten,*" she mumbled against my skin. She increased the speed of the dildo's thrusts only slightly, and I shuddered.

"*Nine.*"

Ray's lips and tongue were ecstasy against me, the heat of her mouth matching the heat of my body.

"Eight."

She was building me to a perfect climax. I was butter under her touch, completely helpless to her heat.

"Seven."

Gripping the bedsheets, I lolled my head to the side and squeezed my eyes shut, concentrating only on the sensation of her tongue flicking over my clit and the sensitivity of the dildo hitting the perfect spot inside me, filling me up as I clamped around it.

"Six."

If Ray wanted me to beg, I'd beg because I don't think I've ever been wetter. My clit throbbed in her hot mouth, and my fingers were aching with the grip I held on the sheets.

"Five."

Panting, I lifted my head to watch her, groaning as her gold eyes met mine. She knew exactly what she was doing to me. Those fucking eyes drove me wild.

"Four."

I didn't know how I could possibly hold out until the end of the countdown.

"Three."

No thoughts anymore, simply one... *fuck.*

"Two."

She increased the speed of the thrusts, and my legs hovered off the mattress as I clenched before she lifted them over her shoulders, getting even closer into me, pressing her nose against my skin as her mouth hungrily consumed me, sucking at my clit until I didn't think I could take anymore.

I couldn't hold out for one more second.

"One."

My orgasm hit me like a punch to the stomach, and I sat up, gripping Ray's hair and pulling her against me as I came. She continued to lick and suck, cleaning up my wetness, swallowing it all keenly.

"Jesus mother fucking *Christ*," I mumbled, slumping back and making her giggle again.

Ray hummed, running her finger between my folds. "You taste so fucking good."

CHAPTER
18

RAY

Letting her have a moment, I simply watched as Ilsa sank back onto the mattress, her entire body relaxing after her peak. I didn't know sex with a human could be like this. I figured I'd only be able to find this sort of satisfaction from other demons. But Ilsa, she was something else, and every layer she let me peel back only intrigued me more.

She stirred feelings in my gut I wasn't willing to admit yet because that was human stuff.

I climbed onto the bed and crawled over her, hovering above her body on all fours until she opened her eyes lazily and looked at me.

Blowing air out of the corner of her mouth to shift a lock of my hair from her cheek, she grinned at me, her smile slowly fading when I didn't return the look but instead continued to watch her. My eyes bored into hers as though we could answer all of each other's questions without words.

"You're a puzzle, Ilsa," I whispered.

She chuckled before that too faded from her face and her brow furrowed.

There was a pause, then she said, "You too."

Ilsa was rubbing my arms now, running her fingertips gently up and down my skin with her nails. The sensation made me shudder, and lust flared in her eyes at my reaction to her touch. How she could induce that effect from me with such a gentle move, I wasn't sure.

So I dealt with it as I normally did with situations I didn't understand—I stopped thinking about it.

As Ilsa sat up, I moved with her, letting her switch our positions before shuffling toward the headboard and resting my shoulders against the pillows as she crawled over me.

There was a mischievous grin on her features as she reached into the bedside table, withdrawing a couple of ribbons. I didn't once stop watching her face as I followed her lead and raised my arms over my head so she could bind my wrists together. The play of different emotions across her face was fascinating, and I bit my bottom lip, unable to tell what she thought as she secured my tied hands to the headboard. She took every motion with such concentration, and when the knots tightened, I smirked.

Whatever practiced knot she was using wouldn't be enough to keep me from her.

When she straddled me, I giggled, tugging lightly against the binds. "You know I could break these easily, right?"

Ilsa tilted her head to the side, a look on her face I couldn't read. "I know..." she said, pausing, a slight smile tugging at her lips, "... but I'm trusting you not to."

The smirk dropped from my face as the impact of her words hit me. "You're... trusting me?"

She ran her bottom lip between her teeth briefly as though she also hadn't considered the full implication of what she had said. When she sighed, it wasn't an angry sound but one of acceptance.

"Yes."

As she stared at me, I felt my eyes blaze yellow for a moment. Another brief moment that revealed my continuing fight to maintain control I was still learning to focus on. Ilsa flinched, but she didn't move away from me. After staring at me for a moment longer, she leaned forward and planted a delicate kiss on my lips—a kiss I returned a moment too late, distracted by the significance of the gesture.

Right before her eyes was a reminder to her of what I was, and she kissed me anyway.

The headboard creaked as I tugged against the binds, groaning against her mouth.

Ilsa grinned. "Don't break them," she whispered. "I promise."

She bent, then lifted my t-shirt and grazed her teeth along the edge of my bra. When I moaned, she returned the appreciation against my skin, the sound vibrating through her lips as she kissed her way along the top of my breasts.

"Harder, Ilsa, please." I wasn't above begging, not when I was teetering on the edge of control. I looked down to find her watching me, her lips still poised above my flesh. Her eyes were swimming with uncertainty, and I simply nodded. "You can't hurt me. I need it, please. Ilsa… *harder.*"

Allowing an open groan of pleasure to escape as she bit into my breast, I arched my back, pushing myself into her touch as much as the restraints would allow. I'd keep my promise. I wouldn't break them, no matter how hard it became. Something about the test to my control was an additional turn-on. I was submitting and in control at the same time, and it was exhilarating.

Ilsa bit harder, and when she drew blood, I moaned in ecstasy, writhing underneath her.

It took me a moment to get my senses back, and I cried out, "Don't taste my blood!"

Ilsa froze, her lips hovering above the wound. There was panic in her voice. "Is it poison?"

I felt the calm rush through me when she stopped—I hadn't warned her too late. "No," I breathed a sigh of relief. "It would start the bonding process."

Ilsa shifted up until her face was above mine and pressed her hand over the wound as though rubbing away the blood would take away what she had done.

"I'm sorry, I didn't mean to…"

"No, it feels good. I want you to bite. But I should've explained about the blood."

"What's the bonding process?"

"Something demons do, it forges a lifelong connection between mates. Between a human and a demon, it would increase your lifespan, give you increased strength and heightened senses." I bit my lip. "It makes being away from your partner physically painful."

"Oh," she said.

She frowned again.

Fuck, she was actually considering it.

It's not that I didn't want to.

Did I?

It was a big step, the most significant thing I, as a demon, could do with another being, and while it was reversible, it was a long and painful process, which would leave us both with scars, physical and otherwise, for life.

"Ilsa…"

She nodded, biting her lip again before grinning at me. I was about to ask what she was thinking when she fell forward onto me, sinking her teeth into my neck, causing me to cry out in surprise more than pain.

My eyes flashed, and my skin rippled. She was enticing a darker part of me.

"*Ilsa...*" There was a warning in my voice this time, and I gripped the headboard to avoid breaking the bonds against my wrists.

"You said harder..." she whispered against my neck, "... so just shut up and take it." She made a trail of kisses down my body again, sinking her teeth into my stomach's sensitive skin, and I bucked my hips toward her, a snarl building in my throat.

The headboard shook.

I'd promised not to break the binds, but I couldn't guarantee the headboard wouldn't crack.

Was she doing it on purpose? Enticing my demon?

She bit along my hip bone and traced her hands down my legs, the touch I had denied her earlier. Smirking, Ilsa took the boots off my feet and dropped them off the edge of the bed. They represented the control I had over her earlier, and the glee shining in her eyes now only reiterated she was in charge now.

I was hers.

Sliding my panties down over my legs before discarding them, she bit me again, drawing more blood. But she was quick to move away, not risking the blood getting into her mouth. After the bite, she had cast me a glance as if asking if what she was doing was okay or for permission to continue. I simply nodded, grateful she took my warning seriously but also drowning in the ecstasy of pleasure meeting sweet pain.

My demon stirred. Part of me ached for her to take my blood, my body screaming in protest as the metallic scent hit my nostrils and was met with no follow-through.

When her tongue ran up between my pussy lips, I cried out again. Looking up over my body, she saw the yellow of my eyes, the blackening of my skin. I was inexperienced at holding my human form when my demon struggled to get out, a skill that could take years to perfect. I needed release, and I needed Ilsa to give it to me because right now, my instinct was fighting against the knowledge I had made a promise.

Above all, I needed her not to be afraid of me anymore.

"Ilsa, please..." I panted. "I can't hold on."

Whether she understood or not, I wasn't sure, but either way, she dived between my legs, licked and sucked at my clit, spread my lips with her fingers, and sucked hard at the bud. I strained against the bonds and struggled to maintain control not to break them. When the headboard cracked, Ilsa's eyes shot up and met mine, her eyelids heavy with lust as her mouth worked against my heat. Driving three fingers into me, she gave me no chance to adjust to the spread and pumped them in and out as she continued to suck at my clit.

Now I was losing control on another level, bucking against her face, my desperation for release evident through the mews and whimpers I couldn't help but let go.

"Ilsa… *fuck.*"

She moved up again, crushed her chest to mine, and continued to drive her fingers into me, the sound of my wet arousal filling the room. When she added the pressure of her thumb to my throbbing clit, I cried out again.

"Shh…" she hummed. "You can take it."

"Yes," I hissed as she added a fourth finger, spreading me wide with her hand and circling my clit with her thumb.

Ilsa screamed when I did. I couldn't contain it.

The ribbon snapped as the headboard broke, and I wrapped my arms around her as I came over her fingers, driving my teeth into her shoulder.

"We did it, we actually fucking did it."

But I couldn't find it within myself to be happy because when I surveyed the scene in front of me, I saw more than the destruction of the terrorist center.

Because that limb, mere feet from me, didn't look as though it belonged to an adult.

How many people were inside the targeted building? The hit had been direct, and it had taken months to find the exact coordinates of the base. They had hidden it in plain sight, and the exchange of weapons was done right in the middle of a once-thriving community.

A community that while quieter, was still active.

Full of innocent people. Innocent people who had copped the brunt of the explosion.

We had been sent in to make sure the threat had been neutralized.

It had been neutralized, all right.

The five men and two women in my unit surveyed the area, kicking over debris.

"No survivors," Darren called.

No survivors at all.

None.

Sand takes on an unusual texture when stained with blood, and I didn't think I'd ever be able to look at it the same again. We had spent a long time in the war zone, where explosions and the crumbling buildings around us were so common it became part of day-to-day life. But this silence was something else. An occasional shuffle as the wind shifted something, the crunch of shrapnel and debris under our boots.

But otherwise, silence.

Maybe this was overkill. Maybe it would've been better to send us in first or use snipers to take out the threats. Those who viewed these zones only through a computer screen from a desk, they didn't want to take the chance that anyone would slip away again, and we'd have to spend more months and lose more lives trying to find them once more.

"There were children here."

My voice was a monotone, unrecognizable even to me.

Vance slapped me on the shoulder as he passed, the strap from my weapon digging uncomfortably into my skin.

"Collateral damage, Ilsa. All part of the game... unfortunately."

Collateral damage.

Part of the game.

Except this wasn't a fucking game.

Was this the moment that would break me? Or was it a slow build of all the incredibly fucked-up things I had witnessed, and even worse, been a part of, finally getting the better of me? People weren't meant to take this. We're not designed to simply keep pulling the trigger without it eventually eating into our minds and souls.

This, I realized, would be my last deployment.

I didn't know what I was going to do, but I knew this wasn't it.

Where would I go? I didn't know anything else. This was all I wanted to do.

But I came to protect innocent people, not harm them.

"Down! Down! Down!"

I responded too slow, too caught up in emotions I should've had a better control on.

The explosion was so loud it left me with nothing but a high-pitched ringing in my ears, so deep it felt like it was within my brain and now embedded in my mind.

Maybe it was.

My vision was obscured by a blinding white light.

Pain, so much fucking pain.

And then nothing.

CHAPTER 19

ILSA

Ray had drawn blood. Her teeth were sharper than I realized, and when she came, she clamped onto my shoulder, punctured my skin, and created a small stream of blood that flooded her mouth. Her lips stayed over my skin, her tongue dancing across the wound. I trusted her to know what she was doing. Obviously, the bonding thing only worked one way, otherwise, she wouldn't still be near the wound she'd created.

Minutes ticked by.

Ray gripped me, painfully hard, with her breathing heavy and ragged. Her eyes were closed and her pupils twitched, darting back and forth underneath her eyelids as though she was dreaming.

When she jerked away from my shoulder, and

her eyes shot open, they were yellow, and I had withdrawn my fingers from her. Her pussy had tightened around my fingers when she came, and it was so fucking hot. She was beautiful in her ecstasy, and I reveled in the twitches of her body and moans against my skin as she came down.

But something was wrong, her pupils still flickered back and forth. She wasn't focusing on anything—it was like I wasn't even there.

She was somewhere else.

Was this normal?

Did this happen last time?

Suddenly, I couldn't remember.

What's normal for a demon anyway?

"Ray—"

"Collateral damage," she whispered, blinking a few times. When her eyes returned to the shades of gold of her human eyes, she was crying, and it shook me.

Such human emotion from a demon. It took me a moment to respond.

"Ray, did I hurt you? Are you okay?"

She shook her head rapidly, but instead of wiping her face, she wrapped her arms around me, crushing me against her and burying her face into my shoulder again.

When she sobbed, I thought my heart was going to break.

"What's wrong? Did I do something wrong?

Please talk to me."

This wasn't a reaction I'd had before after giving a woman an orgasm, and I didn't understand what was happening. Was it different for demons? Did I do something to hurt or upset her?

"Collateral damage," she whispered again. "I understand now."

"What are you talking about?"

"That dismembered arm wasn't the arm of an adult."

Those were my thoughts.

My thoughts.

My back stiffened under her touch, and when I pulled away, she loosened her grip slightly, but not entirely, as if she was afraid I would leave. It took a lot of strength not to. I didn't want to think about what she had said, let alone talk about it. Looking down at her and swallowing heavily, I wiped her tears away with my thumb.

"How did you know about that?" I muttered.

"I saw it."

"I don't understand."

"When I tasted your blood, I saw it. Snippets of a memory like it was my own."

"Of all the memories you could see…" I squeezed my eyes shut, turning away from her.

"We don't choose. If they're strong or prominent memories, they stand out. But always negative ones. Fear, sadness, regret." She released a shuddering sigh. "Back home, it helps when I'm figuring out how to…"

"Torture someone?"

She bit her lip. "Yeah."

Demon.

The word still played in my mind, but looking at her now, I saw her differently. I saw a being trying her best to fit into a world where she didn't belong, trying to find the balance between the rules of the world and her personal boundaries.

It sounded like someone else I knew.

Ray withdrew one arm from around me long enough to angrily swipe away at the moisture on her cheeks. As she hugged me again, I sighed into her touch as she began tracing her fingers up and down my spine.

"I understand now," Ray repeated, and I nodded against her neck. The concerns I had expressed to her, why I had tried to get her to stop what she was doing all along, she understood. Because when you cause destruction, innocents get caught in the crossfire. People in the wrong place at the wrong time.

Collateral damage.

A term that sounded too official and cold for what it truly meant.

I never would've thought I'd connect with another human on this level.

And I certainly never thought I could connect

with a demon.

But apparently, we were exactly what we needed for each other.

How the fuck did that happen?

Strapping a few spare blades to my torso, I pulled my t-shirt down over the bandages. If I got patted down again, there'd be no way they would miss the arsenal of weapons I carried, but something told me this wasn't going to be the same setup Emrick had.

Ray apparently agreed by the way she kept the blades strapped to the outside of her leather pants.

It looked fucking *hot*.

Danger and sex appeal.

I was well beyond wondering what must be wrong with me to consider being with someone like her, knowing what she was. It wasn't news my taste in partners was fucked-up, and usually resulted in destructive relationships that benefited no one.

Except the sex—that was generally amazing.

Although nothing like it was with Ray. She was something else, absolute next-level.

When she caught my eye, she grinned as if she could tell exactly what I was thinking. Which—

remembering she had heightened senses and could read my arousal so well I might as well be holding a flashing sign—she probably could.

Horny. Horny. Horny.

"Keep your mind on the job at hand, *soldier*," she purred.

A shudder ran down my spine at her use of the nickname. In a matter of days, she had managed to shift the meaning of the word *soldier* from the warzone into my bedroom, and I'd be lying if I said I didn't like it.

Because those memories in the bedroom are the ones I'd much rather hang on to anyway.

"Ready to go?" I asked.

"What's his name again?"

I checked the slip of paper. "Earl."

"No surname?"

"None, why?"

Ray bit her bottom lip again. "It has occurred to me..." she started, seemingly carefully choosing her words, "... that he might be like me."

"What makes you think that?"

There was something going on in her mind, something she wasn't telling me, and it struck me like a blow to the head that I had been thinking of Ray as an anomaly. But I had researched this. There were reports from people all over the city from both ends of this towering metropolis, all of which had claimed to have seen or known demons. The place crawled with them, and it made sense the worst of them would be hiding in this part of the city, the darkest part where there was so much to exploit.

Hell, I had seen those eyes in one of the men who had attacked me, so it stood to reason whoever they worked for was a demon too.

I'd been so focused on Ray I forgot to consider the other demons.

"What do we do?" I asked.

"I can handle it," she said, searching my face. "But take a silver knife, just in case."

Pulling a face, I checked my kitchen drawers, unsure if I had any left.

I had one, and I pocketed it.

"Ray?" She hummed, looking up from tightening the straps on her legs. "Why even go through all this? Couldn't you go home or find another city?"

Straightening, she studied me while I got lost in those golden eyes of hers, wondering what she was thinking. "Demons are territorial," she offered. "I came here, now I have a stake in this area, and…" Her gaze swept my body. "It would feel wrong to simply leave. It goes against my instinct."

"Why do demons come to Earth at all?" I asked.

Her slightly sharpened teeth glinted in the light from the small bulb in the kitchen. "Fun, mostly. Some stay because they like it here. While our duties coincide with our instincts, sometimes we need to be... freer. But freedom here means other rules... work, money, all that human shit."

"You're a strange bunch."

She giggled. "You have no idea."

CHAPTER
20

RAY

This was one of my favorite parts.

Apart from the actual fighting side of it, I like the staking out and the stalking, sussing out the layout of the building, finding the weak spots, knowing where the exits were. The thrill of catching someone trying to flee, or even better, *letting* them flee only to cut them off at the exit.

Their eyes would widen, showing the whites of their eyes, the part which held all the fear.

Delicious.

If this Earl character had any security at all, he hid it damn well because there was no evidence I could find of anything protecting him. No cameras or bouncers, no security system, no alarms on the windows. Not even any homemade booby traps.

Nothing.

He must have been pretty confident in himself because this small townhouse which sat in a row with six others, seemed almost entirely unprotected.

We edged toward the border of where the city landscape started to change. Hell, even the roads looked cleaner the further you moved toward the higher side of the city.

Literally, higher. The entire city was on a gentle decline, as though even the world was pointing down to the people who lived in the lower end of town.

The crammed-in apartment buildings started to ease into neat townhouses before stretching into the restaurants and eventually shopping districts, then building back up to high-rises topped with penthouse apartments only the richest could afford. Buildings surrounded by parklands dotted throughout the cityscape as though a few trees and some well-kept public grass could make up for the lack of residential gardens. No one here had gardens—the suburban area was further out from the central business district than most cities. Beyond that, country towns were dotted around and stretched further and further apart until you hit the highway and could take it straight to the interstate.

If you drove for long enough.

This city was a world unto itself.

Earl was watching television in the family room as we peeked through the front window. No curtains or blinds, the muted glow from the screen flickered against the wall behind him. He seemed contented, relaxed almost. Earl was tall—intimidatingly so—his long legs stretched out in front of him, and arms draped over the sides of the armchair, almost brushing the ground with his knuckles, his long slender fingers curved around. There were stacks of items in the corners of the room—technology, blades, guns, cash strewn around. The entire setup reeked of some sort of hole criminals dealt from, exchanging stolen goods.

"Something doesn't feel right about this," Ilsa whispered. I nodded, she was right. None of this spoke of the sort of beings who owned several businesses and would threaten and take lives to protect them. But we needed to find answers, and this was the man who could give them.

"Let's go." I held my hand out, and Ilsa squeezed it briefly before dropping it. She was *on*, in a work mode I hadn't seen of her before, not to this intensity. We had already decided we were going to simply knock on the front door and take him down when he opened it, using my appearance to disarm him.

Because who would be threatened by me? And Ilsa looked too much like a cop. She held it about her, and no matter how much we had practiced pouting and batting her eyelashes, it didn't change anything.

Ilsa pressed her back against the wall next to me as I knocked on the door. I heard a groan from inside as he lifted himself from the chair and watched through the window as he ducked under the doorframe before disappearing from sight into the hallway.

The door opened with a click. There was no chain, not that it would've made a difference.

His face appeared in the crack, gray-blond hair shaved short against his scalp and a long, menacing face.

"Yes?" he drawled.

He caught me off guard. While I suspected it, it was still a lot to take in. Not only was he a demon, he was older than me—much older—and he oozed a dangerous power that flowed through the gap of the open door and spilled into the air around me. Power came with age but so did control, and it felt like he almost wasn't bothering to control himself, his power slipping and sliding around inside him. He reeked of disgust and danger. Not the dark danger Emrick emitted, but the threat of someone who was backed into a corner and desperate.

Slowly, his face changed, his lips lifting into a toothy grin. It wasn't a good look.

"Well, well," he whispered. "Another demon come to visit me for... what, I wonder?"

I forced a seductive smile, hoping it wasn't too late to play my card. "May I come in?"

He nodded, but when he moved to open the door, he grabbed at me, snarling as he moved to yank me inside, his long fingers clasped around my wrist in a vice-like grip. Ilsa came around the corner, kicking the door hard, causing his head to snap back as the edge of it caught him in the face. He released the grip he had managed to get on my wrist. I hated that I wasn't fast enough to move from him, and I had been frozen on the spot again by the simple implication of his power.

He stumbled back into the hallway, his eyes flashing yellow in his rage as we entered the house. Hissing at Ilsa as she stepped into view, he held his long arms open wide, those fingers scraping the walls of the hall on either side of him. He swiped at her like some sort of sea monster from a nightmare, long arms sweeping around in a circle to claim his prey and squeeze the life out of them.

Ilsa didn't hesitate. Jumping on him, I'm sure the only reason she got him to the floor was the combination of his surprise at her attack and her training. Jamming the silver knife into the side of his ribcage, she clasped her hand over his mouth to muffle the roar of pain and anger.

His arms moved to snake around her, but I was ready this time and closed the gap between us as they struggled on the floor. As I grabbed his arms and twisted them behind him, Ilsa helped flip him over onto his stomach. I planted my boot on the side of his face, pressing his cheek into the carpet, his arms twisted and stretched behind him at a painful angle.

Ilsa took the blade from his torso, ignoring the wound it left and cut along his cheek. He roared in rage again, snarling and fighting against our hold on him.

"Why are you trying to kill us?" she cried, holding the blade up in a threat of further pain.

"You didn't come here with innocent intentions. I was protecting my home."

"No," she snarled. "Before today."

He stopped struggling. "I don't know what you're talking about," he said. His voice was a calm drawl again, a heavy, simpering tone that grated against me, and I twisted his arms further.

What was he going to do? Call the cops?

I don't know how he came by this house and the items in it, but from the ill feeling I got from him, I'm guessing it wasn't good. The sense of him was overwhelming—darkness and disinterest—and he had disconnected from both our home world and this one.

"Why are you trying to kill us?" Ilsa asked again. She looked like she would be sick, the color drained from her face. I wondered if she picked up the aura of demonic power around Earl without knowing what it was.

Or perhaps she was frightened she had just hurt and threatened an innocent.

I wanted to tell her not to worry about that, Earl was far from innocent.

"Did Frank send you? That coward can't even do his own dirty work," Earl growled against the carpet.

"Who the fuck is Frank?" I looked at Ilsa, she shrugged, and I eased the pressure of my boot against Earl's face. "You have no idea who we are, do you?"

He laughed a hollow sound devoid of all joy. "No, I don't know who you are or why you're here. But…" he chuckled again, "… I've no doubt I deserve it."

Ilsa tilted her head down, hovering her face above the carpet and holding Earl's eye contact. He looked determinedly at her. All the edge was gone from his posture, and he lay on the floor as calm as if he were about to take a comfortable nap. I didn't let go of his arm, not with Ilsa so close to him, but leaned forward to watch his face as he looked at her.

Nothing, not a flicker of recognition.

"I think we've been set up," Ilsa whispered, standing.

"Well, what do we do with him then?" I tugged on his arm, and he grunted. "He'll retaliate if we let him go."

"I'll tell you what..." he said, and we both paused and looked down at him. "If you tell me who sent you into my home, I won't hurt you."

"How can we trust you?"

"You broke into my house, remember?" He laughed again. "And you sure as hell can't trust whoever sent you to me, either."

Looking at each other, Ilsa raised her eyebrows, and I shrugged.

I'm sure we could both retake him if we had to.

Slowly, I eased the pressure of my boot on his face, and he stayed lying down until I had completely stepped off him. I released my hold on his arm and, in the same motion, pushed Ilsa out of the way, shielding her against the wall with my body. He stood, slowly unfurling himself like the predator he was and towered over us, his head almost scraping the light fitting dangling from the ceiling.

"Coffee?" he offered, dragging the word out around his tongue.

"We're not here to make friends."

"I won't kill you. I live by the same rules you do..." He grinned. "Mostly."

Shaking my head, I didn't break his eye contact, trying to keep his attention off Ilsa and focused on me. She was still standing strong behind me, but this demon, he was a snake in disguise and couldn't be trusted. We were close to the front door. I had made sure not to have him as a barrier between us and the exit. But it would still take us precious seconds to turn and open the door, and we'd have to step toward him as the door swung inward.

"Who sent you?" he asked again. There was no volume to his voice, only a mild curiosity.

I hesitated. "Emrick."

Earl's demeanor changed in an instant. He spat onto the carpet and began muttering obscenities. "That fucking prick, who the fuck does he think he is? Sending assassins into my house and my territory."

"We're not assassins."

"You didn't come here to talk, you made that abundantly clear." His eyes narrowed. "I owe you no explanation, but suffice it to say if Emrick seems to think he's the only one in the city who has a handle on the profits of crime, he's sorely mistaken." He licked his lips, and I felt Ilsa shudder. "Since my previous income… dried up, I've worked my way in with the right humans." His teeth glinted as he smiled again. "Or the wrong ones."

"So this was all some territory squabble?" Ilsa asked.

Earl lifted a slender shoulder in a lazy motion. "Yes. Now, I'll keep my side of the deal, but you better get out of my house. I don't much appreciate being attacked with silver."

He eyed Ilsa over my shoulder, and she stared

hard at him. I smirked. Surely, he wasn't expecting an apology.

Not from my girl.

"Oh shush, it won't kill you." Ilsa shot back at him.

I giggled, and we shared a quick glance. Earl chuckled, and my attention was brought back to him. He waved his finger between us. "You two better be careful, human/demon bondings aren't always approved of."

"Yes, because as a demon, that's what I seek... approval."

His smile dropped. "You better watch your mouth."

Ilsa shuddered again, but she was staring hard at him. "Let's get out of here."

Reaching behind me, I took her hand. "Let's." We kept our eyes on Earl as we backed toward the door, only breathing freely again when we were in the fresh night air and on our way down the street.

Back to Emrick's.

That fucker owed us an explanation.

CHAPTER
21

ILSA

Did the underworld of crime get more complicated because of the involvement of demons, or was it just as dangerous as it always was? I couldn't decide. It seemed fitting if demons were to come to Earth, most of them would choose that path. As Ray so eloquently pointed out, they could release their need for sex and violence in a relatively consequence-free environment.

Free of consequences most of them wouldn't give a damn about anyway. They would be protected by the very organizations they helped serve.

Although, if the bloggers were to be believed, some demons were living it up in legitimate high-end corporations, residing in penthouse apartments, and rubbing shoulders with the cream of society.

Somehow, that seemed even more fitting.

Ray hadn't let go of my hand as we made our way to Urban, and I had considered asking her if she wanted to catch a cab. The club wasn't exactly close. But as much as the long walk would be a strain on my leg, I'd ignore it because walking and holding her hand, I could almost pretend we were normal.

That *this* was normal.

Despite being far from it.

We didn't speak along the way. We didn't need to, and there was something nice about that.

Rounding the final corner, the music from the club was audible, thumping its way down the block. Large spotlights swung lazily back and forth, stationed atop the three-story building, and the purple of the internal neon lights spilled out from the windows onto the pathway, stretching out the shadows of those waiting to get inside.

"They're going to frisk us again," Ray said.

I nodded, but I hated the idea of going in unarmed, even more than last time. Because now we knew, for whatever reason, that Emrick had set us up. Whether he was hoping we'd kill Earl and take him out of the picture, or Earl would kill us, I wasn't sure which.

It hardly mattered.

"I don't think he'll do anything while the club is full."

Ray scoffed. "I wouldn't be so sure of that."

We stared at each other. "I guess we've come this far."

"Wanna go out in a blaze of glory?" Her eyes twinkled, lips twitching with the hint of a grin.

I laughed. "I'd rather not." The smile dropped from my face.

That's what I used to think would be the best ending, what I'd had drilled into me. The only respectful way to go.

But not so much anymore. There was a life to live here, people who needed protection, a growing world of underground crime snaking its way further and further into the city.

My city.

Demons.

I might not be able to protect everyone, but I also couldn't stand by and let everything go to shit either.

All I needed now was a mask and cape.

"I'll protect you," Ray said. She said it with such sincerity, squeezing my hands in hers, I had to chuckle. This woman, this demon, *Christ,* she really cared.

I didn't know why, but she did.

Nodding, we ducked into an alley and relieved ourselves of our weapons, stashing them under a garbage bag. Hopefully, they'd still be there when we got back.

Hopefully, we'd come back.

Striding up to the bodyguard, I straightened my posture, crossing my arms over my chest and keeping my feet slightly apart. *Power pose.* It wasn't accidental. It was a move that showed the definition of my arms, hid my chest, and also hid the limp.

The don't-fuck-with-me expression was purely default at this point in my life.

"We need to see Emrick," Ray demanded of him, and several people nearby stopped chatting and turned to us, not even trying to pretend they weren't listening. The bodyguard eyed us before nodding, unlatched the rope, and let us through. I wasn't sure if it was a good or bad sign.

"You know the way," he grunted.

Things shouldn't be this easy, and if they were, something's wrong.

This thought rightly put me on edge.

But what option did we have?

We'd come this far and needed to see this through. Short of leaving the city and simply hoping we weren't followed, we had no choice.

Ascending the stairs, Ray tried to shove her way past me so she could be in front, but the spiraling case was narrow, and I stood firm. It was a sweet gesture from her but unnecessary. I didn't need her to protect me all the time. Elbowing Ray in ribs as she tried to get past again, we tussled as we made our way up the stairs.

"Stop it, Ray. I can look after mysel—"

"I'm just trying to help—"

"That's very sweet, but let me lead for onc—"

"Let me pas—"

"No!"

"You're so *stubborn*—"

"You can talk—"

We stood at the top of the stairs, wrestling each other in the small space, both trying to lead when the door opened, and the stairwell was flooded with light. Frozen mid-argument, I dropped my hands from Ray's shoulders at the same time she dropped hers from my elbows.

It wasn't the sinister entrance I wanted to make—squabbling like children about who got to go first—but what's done was done.

Striding into the room, Emrick was in the same chair he was last time we were here, only this time he's flanked by two women, one perched on each arm of the chair. He had a hand resting on each of their asses, sliding his fingers under their short dresses, staring at us as we stood our ground in front of him while the door was locked behind us. The women didn't look particularly happy about our presence but stared at us with mingled curiosity and disdain.

Maybe they thought we were their replacements.

Yeah, right.

Ray might look that part, but I certainly didn't. Pretty sure Earl's blood was still on my top. Blood which I noticed Emrick was eyeing. He had the same number of bodyguards in the same positions as last time. Once again, I wondered what was behind the door beyond the balcony.

"Welcome back." Emrick smirked.

"Surprised to see us?" Ray asked.

His lip twitched, and he tilted his head. "Not really, but I didn't particularly care either way. Are you here to repay the favor you owe me?"

"We don't owe you shit. You set us up."

"Ah, you talked to Earl then."

"Yeah, we fucking talked to Earl," Ray snapped. She was becoming agitated, and I didn't blame her, but she needed to keep herself under control.

"Yeah. I didn't think you'd kill him, but it was worth a shot."

"What exactly is your game plan?" I asked.

He stood fast, the girls almost sliding from the arms of the chair as he crossed the room, kicking at the couch in frustration as he made his way to us. The abrupt change in his demeanor was unsettling, and I moved to back away as my shoulders hit Ray's chest.

A bodyguard was between her and the door, and when I glanced at him, he continued to stare straight ahead as though we weren't there and he wasn't blocking the only exit.

Emrick towered over us, his arm muscles visible even through the hoodie he wore, zipper partially open, no top underneath, and his broad chest heaved with his breathing. He'd have been attractive if it weren't for his eyes—eyes so dark they might as well have been black—and hair to match, pulled back into a messy ponytail.

He simply oozed power, and it clicked.

Was he a demon too?

With a swipe of his hand, Emrick shoved me to the side. Ray cried out in rage as a bodyguard caught me when I stumbled on my bad leg, helping me to my feet but then holding me still. Emrick's hand found Ray's throat. I struggled against the bodyguard's hold, but he had me pressed against his barrel-like chest, tree trunks of arms pinning mine to my sides.

"You've been causing nothing but trouble for me, you bitch," Emrick hissed at Ray. His lips were so close to hers. She tried to pull away, unable to wiggle free from his grasp on her neck as the guard behind her took her arms, his knuckles turning white with the pressure he was holding her. Emrick spat on the floor by her feet. "Burning down my buildings... my *bakery*, scattering my workers, destroying pure product, and you thought you would get away with it and simply walk away?"

He licked her cheek, and she recoiled, her eyes flashing yellow, then he laughed. "Don't even think about letting your demon out here, my men will take you down faster than you can blink. Now I *warned* you with silver bullets, and you had the audacity to come strolling into *my* club with your little human fuck toy here."

Ray growled at him, and he laughed again. This time instead of the bark of laughter, it was low and deep, rumbling through his chest and bordering on a growl. He seemed more animal than human, more animal than demon—a feral dog who was angry at the world.

"You failed to kill Earl. While I wasn't holding my breath, it would've been nice to have him out of the picture. But here's the deal..." His voice lost the nasty edge he had taken on and returned to the business-like tone he had used when we first met. "Now, you work for me." He stepped away from Ray, pushed her back against the bodyguard behind her, who shifted his arms and snatched her in a similar hold to the one keeping me restrained.

Emrick approached me, grabbed my hair, and forced me to my knees. I screamed in pain as my leg gave out underneath me, his grip and the pressure on my head so intense I thought he might break my neck.

He could if he wanted to and I knew it.

"Or I'll kill this one," he continued.

Ray went ballistic, fighting against the bodyguard's hold. Her feet lifted from the ground as she tried in vain to throw her weight against the man and push him off balance. Her eyes were blazing yellow, and Emrick tutted and waved a finger at her.

"Keep yourself under control." From his sleeve, a knife slid into his palm, and he held it against my throat while I held my breath. "Or I'll bleed her out in front of you."

CHAPTER 22

RAY

Blood was painfully surging through me, my demon *screaming* to get out, and it was taking almost all my strength and concentration to keep it at bay. I could see Ilsa's throat working against the knife as she swallowed, and my vision switched between the clarity of my demon to human. I didn't care what he did to me, but Ilsa, she was an innocent.

Collateral damage.

"You can't kill her, Emrick, you're bound by the same rules I am." My voice was shaking, and I hated the weakness it portrayed.

His laughter rang out throughout the room. Two of the bouncers, still standing behind where Emrick previously sat, smirked, their shoulders shaking with some joke I didn't understand.

The knife pressed against Ilsa's throat shifted, a

thin trail of blood dripping down her collarbone.

My eyes widened—*he was really going to do it.*

All because of me and my stupid games since I was too inexperienced to figure out a better way to control my demon on Earth. I thought I had it all figured out. I knew nothing and had so much left to learn.

Ilsa's expression hadn't shifted, and I hated to think this wasn't the first time she had been in this situation.

Life or death. Her life in the hands of others.

She trusted me.

"Emrick, please, you can't kill her."

"There's nothing stopping me from taking this human's life, nothing except you."

"*Please.* You can't, the rules…"

The rules I was clinging on to were apparently useless as Emrick continued to laugh at the emotion tumbling through my voice.

What did he want from me?

Was he going to make me beg for her life?

"I'm a fallen angel, Ray. What the fuck else is *He* going to do to me?"

Silence.

"You fell?" My voice was small.

I didn't know. Of course, I felt he was an angel, but I didn't even *consider* he might be fallen.

That would explain the darkness behind his power.

Fuck.

He had no boundaries now.

Ilsa's eyes found mine, and beyond the confusion and fear was accusation. "You knew he wasn't human?"

"I didn't want to freak you out."

Ilsa scoffed, and her expression flared with rage as the knife against her throat was forgotten in the moment when betrayal pushed everything else out of sight. "Oh, yeah, right. *This* would be the thing to tip me over the edge, not you being a fucking demon. Not *fucking* a demon."

"I don't really think this is the time," I mumbled. The ability for her to ignore the pressure of the knife against her throat as it increased with Emrick's impatience because we were having a domestic floored me.

Ilsa's reply was strangled from her throat when Emrick closed his hand around the side of her neck, pressing the tip of the blade into her jugular. "Fucking women, Christ. Shut the fuck up."

"Oh, fuck you, Emrick," I spat.

"You're not in a position to be speaking with such disrespect, bitch."

"What do you want?" I asked desperately.

"You." He slapped his hand lightly against Ilsa's cheek when she went to protest. "You, Ray. I want you. I want your skills, your strength, and your complete disregard for territory and respect. You *will* work for me."

"The hell she will," Ilsa cried.

"She will if she wants *you* to live." He eyed me. "I'll pay you handsomely, and you can stay on Earth, giving in to all your instincts and desires. I'll protect you, so you won't come to harm. You'll have money, power, protection, and anything you want. All you have to do is aim that strength and those fists at the people I tell you to."

Like a guided missile.

"There's no way—"

Emrick shifted his hand until he was fisting Ilsa's hair, tangling it around his fingers and yanking against her scalp, cutting her words off with a cry.

"Shh, human. Let the demon decide for herself."

Ilsa's eyes shot to my face, watering from the pain but filled with determination.

I looked away.

I couldn't face her right now.

Because while she was so steadfast—black and white, right and wrong—I wasn't so sure. Emrick wasn't the good guy, but who was in this world? Was it still wrong to be working for one bad guy against another?

Why shouldn't I work for Emrick?

He was right. I could unleash all my desires, stay here on Earth, earn an income, which otherwise I wouldn't be able to do. I had so much fun taking down all his damn clubhouses, but when I thought

I had it figured out, I had been going about it all wrong. What difference did it make to me who I was unleashing upon? Really, I'd be taking down the same people I had been aiming at before. If they were involved with Emrick, they were unlikely to be innocent people, so my conscience was clear on that front. The only difference would be I wouldn't be harming anything of Emrick's.

It's everything I'd been doing since I got here, but with a wage, and I wouldn't get shot up with silver bullets in the process because I didn't know who owned what.

Bonus.

I wanted to tell myself I was doing it only for Ilsa in some selfless act, but it would be a lie. I had no qualms with lying, but what was the point? He made an enticing offer. Ilsa would be safe, I'd keep doing what I was doing, and all would be right as it were.

"All right."

The silence that rung out after my response was magnified by the grin that lit Emrick's features, somehow darkening his face further as though he had successfully dragged someone else down with him and was proud of it.

He released Ilsa, pushing her forward so she landed on her hands and knees on the floor. She looked up at me, her eyes wide and pleading. "Ray, you don't have to do this for me."

She'd have noticed I couldn't quite meet her eyes—she wasn't stupid. But my mind was made up. "I'm not doing this for you," I muttered.

This was followed by a whoop of laughter from Emrick, and Ilsa stared at me as she pushed herself to her feet, crossing the small room to me as I was released by the guard as well. "What are you saying?"

"I'm not accepting his offer *for you*, Ilsa. I'm doing it because it's a good deal."

"You can't be serious."

"Why not? I get to keep doing what I'm doing, but without consequence, without having to worry about *stepping on the wrong toes* and having people come after me, or you, for that matter. What's the downside?"

"What's the downside?" she whispered. "I thought you understood." Her voice was small, and I stared at the ceiling, rolling my eyes upward to avoid looking at her where I'd have to face the truth. "There are always consequences, Ray. Remember… collateral damage."

When she moved to touch my arm, I wrenched myself from her grasp, unable to take her sensitivity and understanding right now. Ilsa withdrew her hand, looking at me as though the contact had burned her too.

How could she understand? She was only human. I had needs and instincts I absolutely had to get out to keep my demon under control. I didn't want to go back to Hell, not now I knew the pleasures and fun Earth could provide. Emrick was offering me a solution to all my problems, and if all I had to do was be a hired gun, I didn't see the problem.

Ilsa couldn't understand, and I avoided looking at her. Even if I sat her down and explained it to her repeatedly, but she'd never get it. I'd seen her struggle with the morality of my actions since we met, so how could she not see this was basically the same thing? She was judging me by human standards, by *her* standards, and by the image she had built of me in her mind over the past few days. But it wasn't me, not really. I had fallen into the illusion myself, but it couldn't last.

Because I wasn't human, I was a demon.

I didn't have a soul to save.

Except hers.

And maybe Ilsa was better off without me around. Everything that had happened to her was because of me. She was in danger because of me, and she'd had a knife pressed against her throat *because of me.*

This would solve everything.

Except the ache in my chest, which I assumed would go away with time.

"I can't condone this," she whispered. Perhaps she was hoping the audience in the room wouldn't hear.

"What has the world done for you, Ilsa? Used you and tossed you to the side."

"There are still innocent people that need protecting."

I finally met her eyes. I expected to see hurt, but I wasn't prepared for the rage that burned in them.

"I thought *you* understood," I said. "I'm a demon, I'm not like you."

"Pathetic woman, thinking a demon needs her approval." Emrick scoffed.

"Fuck off, Emrick. This doesn't involve you."

He didn't seem at all bothered by the way I talked to him, although one of his guards raised his lips in a sneer at my tone, the one with blond hair cracked his knuckles. Emrick simply continued to smirk, apparently thriving and joyful at the exchange between Ilsa and myself, engrossing himself in the breakdown of what we had built.

Humans and demons—we were too different.

"Are you sure this is what you want?"

Ilsa was offering me an out, one last chance to leave this behind and go with her. But where would that leave me? If I chose her over myself—if I chose us—I'd have to find another way to unleash my demon, to satiate that part of me so I could function in this world, and she'd be in danger again. I didn't know how I could soothe the need for violence without her disapproval. There was no better way than working for Emrick—an income and the freedom to get violent—and Ilsa couldn't offer me that.

"Yes."

Her eyes darted to mine, her jaw clenched against whatever it was she was holding back, expressions or emotions I couldn't predict and probably wouldn't understand anyway.

"Goodbye, Ray," she said, turning on her heel and leaving, throwing the bouncer by the door a glare as he shifted to the side before she disappeared down the stairs.

ILSA

What the fuck just happened?

She went in there with me, figurative guns blazing, ready to take down the bad guy and reclaim her freedom and what she had recognized of her soul, what I had seen in her eyes when she shared my memories, and all the things she had learned about what it meant to be human. I didn't expect her to be human—she was a demon, I knew that— and although the doubts occasionally still swirled in my mind as though I was constantly sorting reality from a dream, I think I had done well accepting her for who and what she was. I had seen her change in the time we were together and had seen snippets of what she was *beyond* the demon, evidence there was more to her than fighting and fucking.

There was a cheeky, intelligent, funny woman. Confident and sexy, protective and yes, even vulnerable at times.

But all she saw of herself was a demon, and Emrick's offer had been too much of a temptation for her to turn down.

Part of me understood, but I couldn't accept it. She knew how I felt about what she was doing from the start, and while I'm aware there are many shades of gray, being in the employ of someone like Emrick was running a mile backward.

Whatever. It wasn't my job to change her mind. She'd figure it out soon enough when she came across the consequences of her work. It might not happen straight away, maybe not for months, but one day, she'd see it, and on that day, I'd not be there to tell her *I told you so.*

Because I would be long gone, gone from her life and this city.

She'd tainted it for me. I had found purpose in searching for her these past few months, and when we were thrown together through circumstance, I had found meaning and comfort in her presence with me as we learned together about acceptance, boundaries, and being more than we thought we could be. I had started to like what I felt and who I became when I was with her—someone who wasn't broken beyond repair, but simply someone who needed one who understood them.

Someone who, as she had said, could read them like a book.

But all of it had been an illusion, part of her seductive nature, and I obviously meant nothing more to her than a convenience at the time.

Ray had chosen her nature over me, and that was okay.

I was okay with it.

Really I was.

Liar.

CHAPTER
23

RAY

Three assignments from Emrick later, and I was feeling pretty damn good.

The ache in my chest hadn't gone away, neither had the throbbing of my clit whenever I thought of Ilsa, and I was irritated that she had awoken something in me I couldn't seem to deal with purely by ignoring it. Eventually, I'd need to satiate the part of my nature that craved sex, but it didn't feel right at the moment. I had no idea why, but I'm sure my body would sort it out. Maybe it was some physical reaction to spending so much time with one human or from my demon coming to the surface and being put back in its place too many times without full transformation.

I didn't care to think about it too much.

Emrick sent me out with his men, so far only to

other clubs in the city, two of which were smaller clubs trying to carve their own territory and encroaching on Emrick's substantial one. The third was a club owned by him, but he had got wind they were skimming off the top and trying to go out on their own.

The rumors were correct, and those responsible were not happy about being taken down a few pegs in front of their employees. We provided an extremely clear warning that next time there wouldn't be the mercy of them being left alive to repent their actions.

Emrick knew I couldn't kill. Unlike him, I was still bound by the rules. But he had plenty of others to take that final step if and when it was required. Again, I didn't need to think about that part of it, I was enjoying myself too much. I had freedom now, more than before. When I had to do my own research and planning—not that there was a great deal of it—it took some of the joy out of the act of destruction itself.

But simply being pointed in a direction, told *go*, and being able to unleash was invigorating.

I am demon, hear me roar.

Emrick was an odd one, and apart from his explosive admission he was a fallen angel when I asked—no begged—him not to kill Ilsa, I had learned almost nothing else about him. The admission might not have meant much to Ilsa, but it was huge. I had no idea what he had done to fall, but it must have been fucked-up because angels don't fall for no reason. Whatever it was, I could see in his eyes he was haunted by it and resented the hell out of his punishment.

Most of my knowledge about Emrick was only what I needed to know—how much of the city fell under his territory. Which, as it stood, was little over one third of the area. Not bad, considering how many others were out there trying to rein some of the territory back into their own smaller operations.

It was so tempting sometimes to ask Emrick what he had done. I really wanted to know, call it morbid curiosity, but I wondered what sort of an angel he was before he fell and what pushed him over the edge.

He wasn't one for talking much.

So I focused on my work, and as I stood with the heel of my boot pressed in the mouth of one of Emrick's employees, I didn't need to think about anything else. He stared up at me, all wide-eyed and innocent as though he didn't know *exactly* what he did to deserve a visit from us. His eyes kept darting to the knives strapped to my thighs, and I'm sure he knew there was no way he could be fast enough to get near them before I pushed my heel through his cheek.

It wouldn't kill him, but it would hurt like hell for

a long while.

"Found it," Tate called from the rear of the building.

He'd been searching for product stolen from one of Emrick's shipments, everything was labeled and accounted for. I'm not sure how these men thought they could get away with stealing from one of the most powerful men in the city with one of the darkest reputations. I asked the man lying under my foot as much, and he mumbled something around my heel. Removing my foot, he spluttered, "P-Please, we'll never do it again."

Tate came up to my side, his presence alone enough to silence the man at my feet. He always wore a long black jacket, looking ever darker in contrast to his white-blond hair like a shadow that flowed around him, making his movements smooth and supernatural. I wondered if the jacket was chosen for dramatic effect or if it was to conceal whatever weapons he carried with him.

Or to conceal his scars if my suspicions about him were correct.

Tate was a demon, I could tell that much, but not like any demon I'd ever smelled before. It was like he was a half-demon of some sort. I had taken a guess once and asked him what had happened to his bonded partner. I had no proof he ever had one, but his scars looked like those left behind when a bonding was broken. I'd only ever seen them once before in person, and I guess in Tate's line of work they added to his menace. Like rope burns, as though he had been bound and the ropes had been dragged slowly and painfully across and around his body, leaving large red welts and marks that snaked across his arms and neck, and I suspected the rest of his body too.

The look Tate threw me when I had asked told me I was on the right track. He smelled like a human infected with demon blood, a bonding gone wrong. Before I could continue the line of questioning about his lost mate, he was at my side, holding a silver knife to my throat.

"You can't heal while silver is in your body, can you? What would happen if I drove this into your jugular then removed your arms?"

"That would be a bit of an inconvenience, I'll admit," I answered, stretching my neck away from the blade.

"As long as we're on the same page." He stalked away, and I had backed off my line of questioning.

For now.

Tate stared down at the man on the floor, his lip lifted in distaste. "Not only will you not do it again, you'll work for free for the next three months."

"You can't... I can't... I need the money."

Tate shrugged, reached into his jacket, pulled out a revolver, and rolled it across his fingers. It was dirty. I didn't know much about guns, but I was certain they were supposed to be kept cleaner than his was. Maybe he had a history with it, a reminder he felt he'd erase if he cleaned it.

Demons aren't exactly known for their nostalgia. But if Tate were human, gaining his demonic powers through bonding, perhaps he was more emotional than his blank expression and hollow eyes let on.

He sneered. "You should've thought about that before you tried to skim off the top. Now..." he crouched, pushing the barrel of the gun to the man's temple, "... I think it's quite clear what your options are here."

"Please," he mumbled, already aware it was useless.

Tate arched a brow at him, cocking the hammer and pressing the gun harder to the man's temple, making him whimper. Tate said nothing further—he didn't need to—the cold metal and his bared teeth spoke for him, and the man simply nodded. He stood slowly, releasing the hammer and placing it back inside his jacket.

"Leave the message," Tate said before he swept out of the building.

Exchanging a look with the others sent on the assignment, the corners of my lips lifted. I liked this part, the part where we *left a message*.

Of course, we wouldn't kill these men. But maybe some way through the beating, they would wish we had.

"Can you shut the fuck up, Ray?"

Glaring at Sven, I then raised my eyebrows at his outburst. We had completed the assignment and were on our way back to the club. It was the point in the night when most of the people had gone home or back to someone else's bed and before dawn broke. The streets were empty and quiet, and I'm sure the grunts and cries of the men we left behind would've carried out into the night. Within these blocks, it's unlikely someone would have called the police.

They knew where their loyalties lay within these streets.

If someone were feeling merciful, they'd call an ambulance.

But that was a big *if.*

"What's your problem? I didn't say anything," I said, sure the confusion was evident on my features and not bothering to hide it. I didn't see the point in hiding my emotions from these men. I wasn't afraid of them, they knew as well as I that I could take them all down. *Humans.*

"You're always humming. You hum when you're kicking the shit out of someone, and I let that slide, thinking maybe it was something that helped get you in the zone. But now you're humming when you walk, and it's getting on my last nerve. Always the same fucking tune."

Staring blankly at him, I asked, "What tune?" I had no idea I was even humming, let alone what the song would be, and for the life of me, I couldn't figure out what he was talking about.

There was a part of me that thought he might be fucking with me, but when Sven hummed a few bars of the song, I stopped walking.

Because it was *her*.

It was still fucking her.

Ilsa.

In my mind, always, never leaving me alone or letting me just be a demon.

The song she had sung so loud and proud while she was taking a shower, the notes she couldn't quite reach wavering on the edge of her voice.

What did she say it was called? "Daydream Believer."

It was the song her mother used to sing to her.

And here I was humming the tune without even knowing. Ilsa was so deep in my fucking mind I couldn't even escape her while I was doing what I loved—beating the fuck out of people who deserved it.

Sven turned when he realized I was no longer following them.

"I have to go," I said.

"What do I tell the boss?"

"I..." I didn't know what to think, but this was messing with my head. "I don't care. I'll sort that out later."

He simply shrugged and turned to follow the rest of the crew as I pivoted and bolted.

Straight for Ilsa's.

CHAPTER 24

ILSA

Days had passed, then a week.

Why did I think she'd come back?

Ray had found her calling, yet I was still waiting for mine. I had found it until the shrapnel had damaged the nerves in my leg, leaving me with a choice—medical discharge or an office role. Working in an office would feel like a punishment, although the consequent eviction from my family felt the same. But that outcome wasn't exactly a surprise to me.

Die on the field or retire with respect.

Walking into Emrick's club had felt exactly like that—if I were to die, it would be with Ray in battle, and if we succeeded, we could retire with respect. Instead, she moved on to her own missions, and I was left in the same hole I was in before I found her.

The room was dark as my computer booted up, and I flicked my fingers across the mouse impatiently waiting for it to start, and then waiting again as it connected to the unreliable Wi-Fi.

Waiting longer for the blog to load.

She'd replied.

The woman I had messaged all those weeks ago, asking for details on where the demon she worked with was located. It felt like another lifetime before I had been tangled up with a demon. Now trying to remember the world I thought I knew before the revelation of her existence seemed like an impossibility.

> *I can't give you that information. If I mention on here where I worked and someone tries to go after him, how do I know he wouldn't then come after me? I've left the city now, but who knows how far their network reaches. It's not worth the risk to give you the business name. I'm sorry.*

Her answer didn't surprise me. Of course, she'd be scared if she'd done the same research I had. She had a boyfriend, therefore something to lose. Whereas I was only on the search for another mission, my next duty. Somewhere to aim my anger and skills at and someone who needed help.

Instead, I found Ray.

Shaking my head of her, I kept reading.

But I can tell you this. Look toward the richest of the rich in the city—those who appeared out of nowhere and rose to the top.

I'm sure her final words on the topic were intended as friendly, but for some reason, they left me with a sense of foreboding.

Good luck.

Good luck, indeed. I'd need the luck if I were to go after another demon.

Tilting my chair back, I stared at the ceiling. Is that what I was going to do? Go after these other reported demons?

And then what?

Would I kill them? I certainly hadn't been pushed that far with Ray.

If all demons are bound by these rules of not killing, why was I fighting them? They'd apparently worked their way deeper into our lives than I could've imagined. In crime, of course, wandering the streets doing what they pleased. In townhouses, in penthouse apartments, in corporations, and in the army. Hell, they were probably in the police force as well. Why not?

Because how far did this go?

And what would happen to me if I exposed myself as knowing about them?

All I was left with was a whole bunch of questions and no answers. I had no direction anymore. Nothing after my discharge felt worthy, and even less so now. I simply couldn't imagine myself going into some nine-to-five job after all this.

Fuck.

Slamming the laptop closed, I stood, the chair sliding out from under me and hitting the wall. Pacing for a while, I stopped in front of the window, looking out over the city as the sun set behind the apartment buildings stretching out into the distance. Shoving my hands in my pockets, I allowed my posture to slump. It was rare I was comfortable as such. I was almost always on edge, but I hadn't felt this lost before. Not once in my life have I not known where I was headed or had a goal and not achieved it. Now, I had no direction, and nothing to strive toward that seemed satisfying to me.

I had nothing.

Do I become some sort of demon bounty hunter? It was hard to imagine. Perhaps I could have before I discovered beyond their nature they had actual personalities—needs and wants, and they knew right from wrong. But even demons were too human to me now, so much so I could barely separate the two in my mind. Because when I thought of demons, all I pictured in my mind was Ray, not some cartoonish image of a red being with hooves and horns.

Although she would look cute in a little headband with horns.

I wondered what Ray was doing now and if she thought of me at all.

Cursing, I turned away from the window. Why should I give a fuck what she thought or was feeling? She obviously didn't about me. She'd found her niche, her place in this world, and I was happy for her. Sort of.

I guess I simply hadn't considered that between the two of us—human and demon—I'd be the one left out of place on Earth.

Several times since she'd been gone, I'd considered drinking myself into slumber, and so far, I had resisted. *My body is a temple* and all that shit—I liked to look after myself. But more than ever, my thoughts tortured me, mingling with those memories from my deployments and recent past. All the worst images and emotions came to the surface because I was left alone with my mind, faced with the potential of a lifetime of this feeling of unworthiness.

Snatching a bottle of bourbon off the counter, I stomped toward the bedroom.

Fuck it! I was going to bed.

And one way or another, I was going to fucking sleep.

CHAPTER 25

RAY

Who the fuck was that?

Crouching in a nook created by an alleyway and a series of bins, I watched Ilsa's apartment building. I could see her through the window, her and some fucking woman who was about to get her fingers broken if she didn't stop reaching across the back of the couch and almost brushing Ilsa's neck as though she wanted to touch or be touched by Ilsa.

Not acceptable.

The growl was working its way through my chest even though no one was around to hear it. What was Ilsa even doing up at this hour? Why did she have another woman over? Was I that replaceable?

Why did I even care?

If I wanted to be critical of the situation, I'd tell myself that technically, I had walked away from

Ilsa, and even though she told me she wasn't happy with the arrangement with Emrick, I had chosen the path anyway.

But that's all *if* I wanted to be reasonable and think this through, which right now I didn't because all I could concentrate on was the possessiveness tearing through my body. All this time I had been defending Emrick's territory when I should've been watching out for my own.

Ilsa was my territory.

My property.

My human.

My mate.

If she'd have me.

Shaking my head, I cleared the doubt because my demon struggled to surface again, tearing at me from the inside. I was getting better every day at controlling it and finding the balance between human and demon. Day by day, I was improving, and over these weeks, I had almost mastered letting out only enough to terrify those who I wanted to experience the fear, yet keeping myself under control. Because when that power oozed through my skin and I started to make humans uncomfortable because they could sense something was wrong but didn't know what, well, it was a powerful tool.

The yellow eyes helped too.

Certainly, I hadn't jumped on anyone else like I

had Ilsa, and I wondered now if it was because I was learning control or if it was her specifically that made me lose it.

So, I waited. I waited for another hour for that woman to leave. Had she been there all fucking night? Ilsa was wearing a tank top and some baggy shorts—her nightclothes. The thought they had slept together only enraged me further.

The woman left, and I followed.

She was pretty, I guess if you like that sort of thing—short, dark hair that bobbed on her shoulders and framed her face and thick glasses that not many people could pull off. She was curvy, legs and thighs that if I cared to, I wouldn't mind biting into.

But right now, she was the enemy.

I hated her on principle.

It didn't take much to get ahead of her. I waited until she passed me, snatching her from the street, and pressing a hand to her mouth as I backed her against the alleyway wall.

"Who are you?" I hissed.

Her eyes were wide, and she was mumbling against my hand. When I moved my hand from her mouth, my other forearm against her chest, pinning her to the wall, she withdrew her hand from her pocket and let me have a face full of pepper spray. I didn't even flinch, and her eyes widened.

Did I *have* to let my eyes go yellow to clear the

spray? No, but it was certainly quicker, and yeah, I guess I liked the fear that flooded her features.

I managed to get my hand back over her mouth before she screamed and started scrambling against me.

"I'm not going to hurt you," I growled, my teeth bared. I tried smiling, but it didn't work, too much anger in my system, and it came out as a snarl. "Who are you?" I asked again.

Dammit! How was I supposed to talk to her if she kept screaming?

Rolling my eyes when she continued to struggle, I slapped her hard enough to knock her out for a bit. I wasn't an asshole, so I caught her as she lost consciousness and lowered her to the ground. Lifting her purse from her shoulder and rifling through the contents, I stopped when I found her identification.

Kelly Michaels, M.E.

So she was the ex-girlfriend mentioned only in passing.

My blood boiled.

Well, that made this *so much better.*

Snarling, I moved to stand and race to Ilsa's when I turned. Grumbling with frustration, I kneeled beside Kelly and lightly tapped her cheek. When she came to, I clasped my palm over her mouth again, sighing loudly when she immediately went to scream.

"Fuck me, woman, I told you I wasn't going to hurt you."

Standing, I pulled her with me, and she continued to struggle against me.

"I'm just trying to… fucking let me… oh forget it!"

Letting her go, Kelly staggered away from me with the force she had been yanking at my grip, and almost lost her footing. She stared at me for a moment, one hand on her head and the other in her pocket, no doubt fumbling with the useless mace. As she bolted, I waved her purse in the air.

"You forgot your—" But she was already around the corner. "Whatever," I mumbled as I made my way back to Ilsa's. I decided this time I better go to her door rather than knocking on the window.

For some reason, it seemed to bother her when I did that.

CHAPTER 26

ILSA

There was a knock on the door just as I was settling back into bed. Huffing with frustration, I got out of bed for the second time that night. If I had left the city when I said I was going to, maybe I'd be sleeping soundly at this godawful hour of the morning.

A lie, but it was a nice lie. A new city wouldn't help me forget the anger and pain swirling in my stomach every time I looked out the window. I had packed and unpacked more times over the past few weeks than I'd like to admit, and each time I was met with the same thoughts.

Where exactly would I go?

Back home? That was a fucking joke.

Every other city would be the same. A place I could afford to stay, and wanted to, would be much the same as this. Something about living in the suburbs amongst happy families didn't sit right with me. As though the combat was part of my blood now, and even if it meant having to be on guard as I was walking down the street to get a coffee, something about that felt more like home than having a lawn and watching small children play in the street as elderly couples went on walks. I had fought so they could have that, but it doesn't mean I had to want it for myself.

And anything resembling home was all I could cling to now because, God knows, I hadn't found anything else in my life that gave me any sort of a sense of purpose.

In the city, at least, there were still fights raging and people who needed protection, a point that had been firmly cemented with my dealings with Ray.

Maybe this city needed me as much as I needed it.

Maybe I'd simply become the vigilante I had tried to stop in Ray.

"Kelly, I told you I'm fine," I grumbled as I approached the door. "You don't need to check on—"

"Hey, lover."

Ray.

At my door.

For what fucking reason?

Slamming the door, I was met with resistance as

she moved her foot in the way and held it steady with one hand. She was strong. Even shouldering the door, I had no chance of closing it.

"What do you want, Ray?"

The anger in my voice was matched in hers—the way she grunted and complained as I tried to shut her out. That only served to make me fume more. *She* walked out on *me,* so what the fuck did she have to be angry about?

"What was Kelly doing here?"

I was no longer fighting the door, but I wasn't letting her in, either, leaning against the wood as it rested on an angle about six inches from being closed while she pressed her face in the gap.

"What's it to you?" I snapped. She thrust Kelly's handbag through the gap, and I snatched at it as I asked, "What the fuck did you do to her?"

"Nothing. She dropped it, and I thought she might want it back."

"Oh? She just *happened* to drop it near you? It wasn't because you did something to her?"

"I only tried to talk to her."

That edge was back to Ray's voice, the one indicating she was fighting to keep her demon under control. Obviously, she had learned nothing about self-control without me. I'm certain Ray wouldn't have killed Kelly, not only because of the rules but because there was still a bit of me hoping she had a shred of humanity and decency left inside her. That some part of the Ray I got to know still existed, even though she had done a full one-eighty when she had gone with Emrick's goons.

"Nice little conversation, was it? Over some coffee and cake?" I asked.

"For fuck's sake, Ilsa, I'm not in the mood for this shit. Let me in."

"You walked out on me. Why should I let you in?"

"Why was Kelly here?"

"What's it to you?" I spat back. "You have no stake over me. Why are you even here?"

She hesitated, and I could see her in my mind's eye biting on her bottom lip. "Because you're a badass, and you're smoking hot."

"Not good enough."

"Because you're my best friend?" Ray offered quietly, her inflection rising at the end of the sentence.

I couldn't help snorting. "I'm your best friend?"

"Fine. You're badass, you're hot, *and* I like you."

"Ray..."

"*Fuck,* Ilsa, you're going to make me say it, aren't you?"

Grinning, I leaned my head against the door, glad she couldn't see how much I was enjoying having the upper hand on her. I wanted to stretch this out. She deserved it for making me care for her then leaving the way she did. The pain was still thick in my chest, a throbbing reminder of how she had made me feel and what it felt to have that illusion of *us* shattered. There was anger there. Of course, there was, and I was trying hard not to overthink how quickly my anger had evaporated as I heard the frustration in her voice when she realized I was messing with her.

She was my purpose.

Fuck.

So, I waited.

"You're badass, you're hot, and…" she took a shuddering breath, "… you're a good person, Ilsa, and I don't know how to do that. I am what I am, and I can't change that, but I *want* to do better…" She paused. "You make me want to do better."

The final words were delivered through gritted teeth, and I could hear the edge to them.

Slowly, I straightened, relinquishing my weight from the door and resistance to her trying to push her way into my apartment. But the door stayed as it was. She had stopped trying once I had moved and was no longer forcing her way into my apartment.

Or into my life.

I'm not a fool. I know how much it would've taken from her to not only come to the realization she did, but to say it out loud. It took a certain level of willpower not to laugh when I stood to the side and pulled the door open, watching her standing there on the threshold, jaw tense and eyes boring into mine.

Golden eyes, not yellow.

She was keeping herself under control for me.

"May I please come in?" she asked curtly.

I smiled then. I couldn't help it, and instead of smiling back, this only made Ray's jaw tense further as she gritted her teeth against giving me a piece of her mind for making her talk openly about *feelings*. Oh, what torture that must have been to tell me her emotions.

"Of course, you can," I said as sickly sweet as I could manage.

Stepping to the side, Ray swept past me, and I closed the door with a quiet click.

The moment I turned to face her, she was on me.

We lay there on the floor, not having moved far from the door since I let Ray into my apartment. My shorts were around my ankles, and Ray's pants were open and yanked slightly down, the waistband sitting underneath the curve of her ass. Panting slightly, I swallowed heavily and rolled my head to look at Ray. She had her arms folded behind her head as though she didn't have a care in the world. But as I watched, a slight frown formed on her face, subtle twists to her expression as she worked her way through whatever she was thinking.

She had jumped me the second the door was closed, and I absolutely did *not* have the willpower within me to fight my desire for her. We came together, our hands shoved down the front of each other's underwear, and when she forced her fingers into my mouth, making me taste myself, I returned the gesture.

Fuck, it was hot.

I was about to ask what she was thinking when she rolled her head to me, the intensity of her gaze taking my breath away and, for a moment, the flash of bright yellow passed across her eyes.

"Why was Kelly here?" she asked.

The anger from her earlier accusation had evaporated, resignation heavy in her tone, and I know which side of her I preferred. This quiet voice, the pressing of her lips together as if to stop further questions escaping, didn't suit her. Ray was loud and proud, and I liked her like that.

I wanted her just as she was.

"She was worried about me."

"Why? Did you call her? Did she stay the night?"

My eyebrow quirked at the same time I chuckled as her questions all tumbled out once the dam of self-control was broken. Reaching out, I rested my hand on her forearm. "She finished a late shift and stopped by to see me. I didn't call her."

"Why was she worried about you?"

"Kelly was providing me with police reports when I started trying to track you down, as you know. The lack of evidence was further proof to me you weren't human." Ray smirked, pride evident, and I rolled my eyes before continuing, "I hadn't been in touch with her since I found you, and she was worried I *had* found you, or maybe you had found me first, and I had been injured or killed."

"What did you tell her?"

"A version of the truth." I sighed out loud, blowing my hair from my face. "I told her I had lost interest, that I had been chasing a ghost and wasting my time, and I felt my chase for you was simply some way of trying to make myself feel needed and useful again."

"And that's the truth? What you told her?"

"Parts of it."

"You're useful to me," Ray whispered, pouting when I laughed. I didn't mean to, I knew what she meant. "I saw her with you through the window," she continued. "She looked like she was flirting with you. It made me crazy."

"She *was* flirting with me."

Ray sat bolt upright. "I'll kill the bitch."

Laughing again, I sat up too, slower than she had and rested my hand on her leg, tracing small circles with my fingertips. It felt good to touch her again. Waiting until she looked at me, I said, "I turned her down, Ray, in no uncertain terms. Besides, it seems you may have scared her away for good."

"Good," she growled.

Getting uncomfortable at the twist of fabric around my thighs, I pulled my shorts back on and Ray followed suit. After a beat, I asked, "Will Emrick come after you?"

Ray shrugged. "Probably, but I'll deal with him when he does."

There was that wicked grin again, and I didn't realize how much I missed it. Making even a dire situation seem like it was all one big game, and I supposed to her it was. Life on Earth was new and exciting to Ray, finding her place in a world she was still exploring the limits of. Maybe we could make a game of life together. It sure would be a nice change of pace for me. We sat in silence for a moment before Ray turned to me, and I was lost in her eyes again.

Someone, please tell me how this happened. How I found myself tangled up with a demon, how I ended up falling for that demon, and how she turned out to be everything I needed.

The brightness in my life that was otherwise dark.

Fuck.

Guess Ray really did brighten my night.

Smirking, I looked at her again. I wanted to point out how her little joke turned out to be true, although uttering such words out loud still felt like a big step. It was one thing to attack each other physically and fuck until we fell into exhausted heaps, but to tell her how I *felt?*

Surely, she already knew. I knew it was hypocritical to force that confession from her and then hesitate myself about the same thing. But she had walked out of my life, the least she could do was suffer some discomfort while she groveled at my door.

Ray wasn't smiling, and that made the grin fall from my face.

Then the yellow passed across her eyes.

"Are you still having trouble containing your demon?" I whispered.

Her eyes flashed again. "No," she muttered. "I'm much better at it now."

"Then why..." my voice trailed off when her expression darkened, and I knew I was in trouble.

But I liked this kind of trouble.

Her lips met mine, and I took my time running my tongue over them, taking in the feel of her, the curves, the taste, and everything about those lips, memorizing them against mine. She let me take her mouth slowly, gently, until the telltale rumble started in her chest, the growl moving up her throat until it vibrated against my mouth. When I opened my eyes again, hers had changed to yellow.

"You haven't been giving in to your instincts enough, I see. All fight and no fuck?"

Her eyes flashed, and she bared her teeth. "No." There was the supernatural edge to her voice, the one that should induce fear, but right now, the rumble in her chest only made my clit throb. "There's been no one but you." I trembled, and she took a deep breath like an animal sniffing out its prey, and her eyes flashed again, the yellow having taken over completely and the irises becoming black slits against the color.

She was letting go on purpose.

"But I'm about to." She hissed out the words.

I wasn't going to make it easy for her.

Ray pounced, and I rolled to the side, coming up into a crouch position and pivoting to find her mirroring my defense. She had one leg stretched out, the other bent underneath her. From that position, she could attack or defend. No prizes for guessing which path she was about to take. Ray bared her teeth at me, and for a moment, only a split second, I doubted what I was doing because she looked downright dangerous. But beyond the hiss, there was an unmistakable grin there.

What the fuck was I doing teasing a demon?

But this thrill, this danger, it pulsed through my veins. Somewhere deep inside me, I knew ultimately, I was safe, that Ray couldn't—and wouldn't—kill me.

But still, this game was fun.

It was *my* turn to fuck with *her*.

Ray pounced, and once again, I rolled, but she was ready for me this time. She reached out and snatched at my arm, breaking my roll, and slammed me onto my back before dragging me toward her. I could see the pops of black ink dotting her skin, spreading. I knew I couldn't keep this going forever, that I was further testing her newfound control.

But she wanted to do better.

She wanted to be challenged to be a better person.

So, I thought, *do better, Ray.*

Staying still as she leaped on top of me, I couldn't help the shriek of joy that escaped my lips as she tore my t-shirt from my body, shredding the fabric before leaning down and sucking at my nipples. I almost forgot myself, lost in the ministration of her tongue—*was it slightly more pointed than it normally was? Longer? Christ*—before I regained my senses.

I went for the eyes.

As she sat up and hissed again, angrily swatting my hands away from her face, I managed to roll onto my stomach and began belly-crawling away from her.

But I didn't get far as she grabbed my ankles and yanked me toward her.

"Try that again," she whispered against my ear, crushing my body to the floor with hers. "I dare you."

Even as she pressed on the back of my head, and her nails tangled in my hair, I still laughed as my cheek was pressed against the carpet. "I give up," I cried, my fingers splayed on the floor next to my head in surrender as I tried to keep the laughter from my voice, failing and causing her growling to intensify.

"*Good.*"

Staying on my stomach as she tugged down my shorts and underwear and discarded them, Ray snarled as the fabric got tangled around my ankle. I spread my legs without her having to guide me. I was already wet, waiting for her fingers and tongue.

That tongue—I'm sure it was longer than it was when she was in full human form.

Oh God, it was all shades of wrong that it turned me on.

Ray drove two fingers inside my warmth, keeping her other hand firmly on the back of my head and her breath hot against my ear. There was no mercy, no warm-up, but there didn't need to be. Whether it was from what I felt for her, or her demon instinct, or a combination, I was so wet I was dripping onto the carpet before she had even touched me.

I didn't care what the reason was anymore for

my response to her because I knew this was something real.

She groaned as she fingered me, curling and twisting her fingers, hitting all the right spots inside me as I squirmed and ground my hips against the floor. It was her turn to laugh now, knowing I was completely at her mercy.

"Beg me, soldier," she crooned against my neck. "Beg me for release."

I could barely think straight, let alone summon the words to beg.

"*Beg*," she snarled.

"Please," I panted. "Please, Ray, please, make me come. I want to come around your fingers, I want your tongue, your hands, your pussy, everything. Please let me come."

She chuckled, and in one swift motion, removed her fingers from me, shifted down and spread my thighs with her hands, and tongued me. I cried out, the sensation unlike anything I had experienced before. Her tongue *was* longer the closer she got to her demon form, and as it snaked inside me, lapping at my juices, an orgasm exploded from me as she added pressure to my clit with her fingers. The slightest touch on my throbbing clit, and I was over the edge, writhing and squirming, unable to decide if I wanted to pull away from the assault and pleasure or push toward her.

Her fucking tongue, I wondered if it got even

longer when she fully changed.

There was something definitely not right about me desiring that.

But right now, I didn't give a fuck.

As I came down from my high, Ray shifted away from me, and I took a steadying breath to clear my head. Flipping me onto my back, Ray removed her pants and crawled over me again, not stopping until her knees were either side of my head. Tucking my arms around her thighs, I gripped her ass, spanking her once, *hard,* how I knew she liked it. I smirked as she grabbed my hair with both hands, tangling her fingers and yanking my mouth toward her pussy.

"My turn, soldier."

EPILOGUE

RAY

Four Months Later...

Her eyes glowed yellow, and I won't pretend I didn't love it when she did that.

Ilsa was a fast learner, and she had learned to focus her inner demon instincts a lot faster than I had when I came to Earth. But then again, Ilsa had a lot more self-control than I did, in general.

If anything, I've learned that.

It was still something I liked to try to break—her control—to see how far I could push her before she lost it, and this was one of those days. I had aggravated her enough, her eyes flared yellow, not quite enough for the pupils to change into the black cat-like slits, so she still hung on to whatever thread of control she had left.

Smirking, I knew I'd break it.

If anyone could annoy her enough to make her lose her fucking mind, it was me.

And yes, I said that with a level of pride.

"Is that all you've got?" I goaded, her lip lifting in a snarl at my resulting giggle.

"Fuck you, Ray," she cursed.

"Later." I winked at her, which only irritated her further. She wasn't in any sort of mood to be dealing with my shit right now.

If that wasn't an invitation to keep doing it, I didn't know what was.

I had about half a dozen things I could say, ready and waiting, which would push her over the edge, but I didn't get the chance. She launched at me, slammed her palms into my shoulders, and knocked me off my feet. Laughing, I used her momentum against her and continued the roll, pulled her over me so I ended up on top of her, crashed her back against the floor, and pinned her down. The growl she released was animal, and I giggled again. Perhaps she didn't have the level of control she thought she did.

Ilsa only seemed to be in control of her demon when she was in control of the situation. Take that away from her, and she became more animal than woman.

And I loved it.

Two months ago, we had bonded, the process of becoming mates. She was hesitant to drink my blood, sure she was going to get some of my memories the way I had hers. But it didn't work like that. Only demons had that reaction to humans—not even with other demons did it work. It was a tool to induce terror and learn what we needed to about our human victims, nothing more.

After the second time of drinking my blood, we were bonded, and I had to teach her to control her inner demon the way I'd had to learn when I came to Earth. Something I had to focus on harder since I'd decided to stay. There was nothing for me in Hell. Nothing like Ilsa.

Now, she was stronger, more powerful, her senses sharpened, and her lifespan extended.

She was mine, and I was hers.

Just how I liked it.

After leaving Emrick's employ, my concern was I wouldn't be able to keep my bloodlust and need for violence controlled. But after the bonding, the solution presented itself to us.

We fight each other.

It led to better sex too.

Emrick stopped giving a shit when I stopped tearing apart his clubhouses. Tate said he didn't trust me anyway, which was fine, because I didn't trust any of them. The issue wasn't gone forever.

I'm sure I was now on some low-key shitlist of Emrick's. It didn't bother me much, though it bothered Ilsa. I could tell by the way she pursed her lips when we went near the club or his name was mentioned.

He'd come after me one day, I was sure of it.

Wasn't he in for a shock when he came across my new Ilsa?

Wrapping my fingers around Ilsa's throat, I goaded her some more. "Come on, soldier, you should be able to control yourself better than this."

She hissed at me again. The more frustrated she grew, the sloppier her skills became. The more mistakes she made during a fight, the more shit I gave her about it. It was a vicious cycle, but if she was going to lecture me about keeping control, then she better get used to me pushing her buttons until she lost it. What's more, I loved how freely she gave into the newly acquired demon side of her, the way she openly let it mold to her body rather than fighting it. I'd heard bonding could be difficult on humans sometimes, on the rare occasions I had heard of it occurring. But Ilsa was perfect, in more ways than one, and her training and self-control lent itself perfectly to learning how to handle her new powers.

Ilsa tried to move me off her using the same maneuver she had when we first met, and I had her in the same position, but despite her increased strength, it didn't work this time. She settled for going limp, perhaps hoping I'd let up on her.

Fat chance.

When I continued to increase the pressure on her neck, her eyes flashed again, and her hands flew to my wrists, sinking her nails into my skin until she drew blood. Leaning forward, I licked a droplet of blood off my skin before pushing my tongue into her mouth. She fought, but her hold on me relaxed as she moaned openly into my mouth.

"That's not the instinct we're currently working on," she whispered against my lips.

"Oh?" I mumbled, kissing my way along her neck. "What makes you think you're in charge here?"

She got me this time, wrapping both legs around my waist and flipping me over. While she hadn't regained full movement of her injured leg, it was certainly much better than it had been before the bonding. Demon's accelerated healing had allowed some of the damaged nerves to heal, and she had regained almost full mobility.

When Ilsa leaned over me, I thought she was going to kiss me again, but she simply hovered her lips over mine, driving me wild with her scent. Lifting herself off me, I grunted as she used my shoulders to push herself upright before dancing across the room, waving her ass at me in a tease that was meant to enrage.

It did.

When I growled at her, she chuckled, knowing she had turned the tables. All my teasing and big talk were lost the moment her lips were on mine, and I tasted her again. It made the fight seem pointless when all I wanted to do was take her pants down and have her naked in front of me—or under me, or on top of me—I didn't care. I simply wanted her to be naked.

Perhaps Ilsa understood the importance of these fights more than I, or perhaps she simply enjoyed the fact if she kept it going and kept pushing me to fight with her when I had lost interest, that I hate it.

It was probably revenge for all the times I gave her a hard time, which were a lot, and it wasn't going to end any time soon.

Ilsa crouched into a defensive stance, her body turned partially to the side and her head tilted down. I could see the sweat glistening in her cleavage, the tight black sports bra hiding nothing from me. Her eyes had returned to their natural and beautiful brown, but the twinkle in them told me she was far from done.

"You ready?" she asked.

"When I get you..." I hissed, "... you know I'm going to tear your clothes off, right?"

She grinned. "Bring it on."

And when she beckoned me with her finger, I was on her.

The END

Next in the Unearthly Sins Series
Dark Angel

ACKNOWLEDGMENTS

I'll say to myself, *this time I think I'll keep my acknowledgments short*, but then as is my way, I'll ramble for a bit, forget my point, and come around in a big circle.

Thank you again, Kate and Chris. There were some interesting and hilarious discussions surrounding this particular book, and it was great fun to bring it all to life.

To Nicki, Kaylene, and Kimberly. You're awesome, and I'm thankful and ridiculously grateful for you.

To Mum, who insists on owning and reading all my books—just skip over *those* parts, okay?

Jason, even as an author, I can't find the words to express how amazing you are, so I'll simply say thank you and hope that you already know what I can't fully express. x

CONNECT WITH ME ONLINE

ANGELS AND FIRE BOOKS
Find our exciting stories at:
www.angelsandfirebooks.com.au

READER GROUP

Want access to fun, prizes and sneak peeks?
Join my Facebook Reader Group.
https://www.facebook.com/groups/588038442170571

NEWSLETTER

Sign up for my Newsletter.
https://www.subscribepage.com/angelsandfirebooks

BOOKBUB

https://www.bookbub.com/authors/stefanie-dawn

GOODREADS

Add my books to your TBR list
on my Goodreads profile.
https://www.goodreads.com/author/
show/21761217.Stefanie_Dawn

AMAZON

https://www.amazon.com/author/stefaniedawn

WEBSITE

http://www.angelsandfirebooks.com.au/

INSTAGRAM

https://www.instagram.com/angelsandfirebooks

EMAIL

info@angelsandfirebooks.com.au

FACEBOOK

https://www.facebook.com/stefaniedawnwriter

About THE AUTHOR

Stefanie Dawn has been a writer and creative soul all her life **and** strives to give her readers stories they can escape into as they become absorbed in the worlds created.

When she isn't writing, Stefanie might be painting, reading, or watching movies. She loves the process of producing films as another form of storytelling. There's also a good chance she'll be baking some delicious treats—pretending she won't later regret consuming them—or simply enjoying a cocktail with friends.

Stefanie Dawn lives in South Australia with her ever-supportive partner and a lovable gang of rescue cats.

Lure of a Demon

You can stay up to date with
Stefanie and her books at:
www.angelsandfirebooks.com.au